Roma Tearne is a Sri Lankan-born, Oxford-based artist, film-maker and writer. She trained as a painter, completing her MA at the Ruskin School of Drawing and Fine Art, Oxford.

Her debut novel, *Mosquito*, was shortlisted for the 2007 Costa First Novel Prize and 2008 LA Times First Fiction Award. *Brixton Beach* was a TV Book Club Best Read and *The Swimmer* was longlisted for the Orange Prize in 2011 and Asian Man Booker in 2012.

Praise for Roma Tearne:

'Tearne brings her skills as a painter to her writing'
Sunday Telegraph

'Roma Tearne is one of those writers who manage to interweave the political and personal to tremendous effect'
The Independent

'Tearne captures the desperation, fear and hope of love during wartime'
Publishers Weekly

'Prose so lush it appeals to every sense ... Roma Tearne is an exquisite writer and captivating storyteller'
Aminatta Forna, author of *The Memory of Love*

D0416859

The White City

Roma Tearne

AARDVARK
BUREAU

The White City

Roma Tearne

Aardvark Bureau
London
An imprint of Gallic Books

An Aardvark Bureau Book
An imprint of Gallic Books

First published in Great Britain in 2017 by
Aardvark Bureau, 59 Ebury Street, London SW1W 0NZ

A CIP record for this book is available from the British Library
ISBN: 9781910709429 [HB]
ISBN: 9781910709337 [export PB]

Typeset in Garamond Pro by Aardvark Bureau
Printed in the UK by CPI
(CR0 4YY)
2 4 6 8 10 9 7 5 3 1

For The Disappeared.

... there is no likelihood of our being able to suppress humanity's aggressive tendencies.
Sigmund Freud to Albert Einstein 1931–1932

1.

Finally, after twenty-seven years, the ice is melting. But, in this devastated city with its once-commercial wharves and gleaming Shards, its empty cathedrals and ivory minarets, no one notices. Life amongst the ruins goes on in the same hopeless way and the pulse of existence seems lost. The half-buried homes, the outlines of trains standing motionless on frozen railway tracks, the useless street lamps and the iced-up car parks all remain abandoned. I am used to this; to the silence of ice, its cruel beauty, its gothic, petrified grandeur, and so, for a few weeks, I, too, notice nothing. And then, unexpectedly, a faint shimmer of water forms across the horizon and I realise: the blue ice is melting.

Every day when I stand on high ground and look towards the Tower, to where the river used to be, I see it melt a little more. This blue ice lies deep beneath the frozen world. When the earth starts to warm up, the blue ice shifts and the white ice on top cracks, bends and splinters with a ferocious pyrotechnic energy. Watching, I can't help but be astonished. The cracks are thin and appear as delicate geometric folds drawn on transparent paper. Underneath it is possible to see glints of greyish water moving with deceptive calm. But this situation is becoming increasingly lethal, for the water is actually fast-moving and deep. At first there doesn't seem anything dangerous but then one of the guards walking across the river gets trapped between two of the ice plates and when his companion tries to save him another chunk of ice breaks off and they both vanish under it. There is a brief thrashing of arms in the undertow and then the crunching and grinding of the huge sheets of ice. The river is alive and seems to be digesting the men. I watch all of it standing by the bridge. Even if I wanted to I am too far away to help them. Soon after, other men who used to skate across the river, frightened away no doubt by what has happened, disappear. News travels surprisingly fast in this static, empty city.

So, yes, the river is slowly returning to its former state. Daily I see its curve widen like shot silk across the horizon. There are no trees in this part of the city. Only cranes and unfinished skyscrapers rise alongside empty office blocks. The world, mute for so many years, is now filled with sounds of fracturing ice, brittle and unpredictable. It is impossible to tell where the next fault line will appear.

On one of my morning walks I go as far as the Tower itself. This ancient prison both fascinates and horrifies me.

'Where are your prisoners now?' I shout.

My voice is whipped away by the wind. There isn't anyone to hear me. There are no ravens any more either, but a blackened, ragged cloth still hangs at half-mast. I move closer, hesitating, staring at the broken bridge, once such a symbol of greatness in this place. Then I notice that even in the moat the ice has broken. *Water!* Grey, dirty; but still, water.

Walking across this white desert isn't easy any more. The sky has lightened but the wind remains bitter. In spite of it though, today, I walk for three hours. I am a swathed figure dark against the whiteness of the city. Occasionally my long, still-black hair escapes and flies with the wind. I am the raven in this birdless world. Ahead of me I notice other figures huddling together. One holds up a large black cross. From this I gather a funeral is taking place beside the river. Soon someone will dig a hole, or if not dig then find a gap between two ice cracks and the body will be pushed in. Death and water go well together, I suppose. There is nothing remarkable in such an event. I skirt around the gathering and turn away from the river.

I decide to visit the wrought-iron ruin, once a huge exhibition hall, now crystal-white and encrusted with icicles that sparkle like chandeliers in the uncertain light. Afterwards I walk for so long and in such an erratic manner that eventually I come to a series of old railway arches. I have been here before on a different occasion. Usually there are huge stalactites hanging down from its arches but today they appear shorter and the ground is wet and slippery. A single icicle breaks off with a brittle snap, narrowly missing me. As I walk past I notice a small white sign on a wall.

The Cut, I read.

And then in red letters, *S.E.*

On the way back I fall over because the thawing ground has become glassy and dangerous. I fall into a ditch. When I stand up I am soaking wet. Water! Again. Lately I have seen marks appearing all over the once-smooth ground. When I first noticed this I was puzzled but after a while I realised these marks are the tread from tyres of old, obsolete grit lorries. Preserved like fossils. There are no moving cars, of course, just rusting body parts embedded in the ice, emerging daily into view in a fragmentary way.

Yes, the thaw has finally come.

I am almost home when I see something so horrific that I feel a jolt like electricity passing through my body. Trembling, I am compelled to move closer; to look. And what I see is a man, fully clothed, slumped in his car. Preserved in ice, complete with tie and suit, his face embalmed by refrigeration. Perfect features, perfect skin, perfect hair. Dead. Above him, a sign showing faintly through the dissolving veil of ice.

Car Wash, I read.

I hurry back, hardly noticing the flat roofs of the buildings that are appearing, hardly caring that once, long ago, this was a street full of shops, cafés, homes. In the descending pink-streaked twilight I pass a man trying to roast rats over damp wood. I wonder how long it will be before he finds the body in the car.

I reach my house. It is the very same house where I was born and spent most of my childhood. Where Aslam, my brother, too, was born. There isn't much that resembles our old home. I burned most of the furniture before discovering other methods of keeping warm. In the kitchen I stand for a moment staring out of the window. The high banks of frozen whiteness in the back garden have been creaking and expanding for weeks as though they were a large wooden ship. The thaw is speeding up; I am aware of a change from this morning, even. The top of the old shed has become visible and suddenly, out of some long-forgotten place, comes the memory of those things that I thought were buried for ever.

A lawn mower for a lawn that no longer exists.

An old prayer mat for all those unanswered prayers.

Computer parts belonging to my brother, Aslam.

A tool kit my father used for boarding up a window.

The pram in which our mother pushed each of us.

A cool box.

At the thought of the cool box I begin to laugh but my laugh changes almost instantly. What comes out of my mouth now cannot be called laughter. Staring at the darkening garden with its buried, abandoned things, I remember the love song you once sang to me when I asked too many questions.

Why tell them all the old things ... buried under the snow

I continue to stare blankly out of the window, hearing your voice, tenderness never far from the surface. And then I hear the thud of ice falling somewhere out of sight. I jump. And I realise there are other sounds rising and falling above these cracks and explosions. Sounds so small yet unmistakable. Small drops of water are beginning to fall from the eaves.

There is no doubt about this thaw, I think again.

Something on the shelf of my heart shifts as, through the high banks of frozen whiteness looming out of the night, I see the beloved faces coming towards me like revellers after a drunken party. Yes, you are here, demanding to be acknowledged. So that, going out into what passes for the back garden, I notice the Milky Way has flung its stars far and wide like jewels across the sky. And as the rain begins its insistent tattoo across the windowpane I see I can no longer ignore the past.

15

2.

When it began it was still winter in the white city. After the park disappeared and the lake froze the whole place seemed to lose its way. Everywhere you looked you saw leafless trees, their white arms petrified and still in the blurred air. The winter sun was cold and very low. Small starving birds came without sound to the feeding ground in our ghost-garden, which in time began turning into a graveyard. Ice had begun to form and unfurl its white foliage in gutters and hedges. Winter had begun in October and it was now July. As yet there was no sign of summer. Occasionally the snow would turn to sleet but then return again. The weather forecasters promised a warming but no one believed the weathermen any longer. Each day the blizzards got worse and each day the grey clouds were oppressively static and low. The temperature continued to drop sharply. One degree below freezing, five degrees, then minus ten. I had decided to pay Calypso and Hektor an overdue visit.

I had been in a state of confusion. A year earlier I had met a man who, even in my limited experience, seemed a little crazy. He both mesmerised and infuriated me. Yes, Raphael, I am talking about you! You were the person I was in danger of getting too involved with. Because I was training to be an artist, I'd started to draw you – but now I was fed up, on the verge of chucking it all in, moving to another country, and beginning again. Such was my uncertainty I thought I might confide in Calypso. But of course, because of what followed, that confession never happened.

On the day I speak of, Calypso had been walking back from the outdoor market, carrying two plastic bags bulging with vegetables. She felt lucky, for vegetables were getting harder to come by. With the scarcity of bees – no government had stopped the use of pesticides in spite of all the protests – some plants had died out. But on that day Calypso had bought what she could. Her bags were about to split. She was thinking of something else and not taking much notice of her surroundings. She was also singing to herself, as was her habit. So she'd reached her front door before she saw what was going on.

'Hey!' she said in her honey-deep voice. 'What d'you think you are doing?'

The pavement was crowded with people: police, a motorbike on its side and a helmet on the ground. Her first thought was that someone had had an accident outside our house. Then she saw the front door. It was swinging on its hinges and you could see right through into the hallway: the stairs with the coats piled on the banisters, some trainers kicked over, odd socks drying on the radiator and a drum of oil that should have been in the cupboard but was still beside the stairs. You could see all the way into the kitchen too. The light inside was diffused, pearly, whitish. That was when she screamed.

Someone pushed her roughly out of the way and one of her plastic bags ripped. A cabbage rolled onto the ground. Like a head. Her umbrella had turned itself inside out in the wind so she abandoned it and bent to pick up the cabbage instead. The snow blew into her face.

'Don't move, madam! *Madam*, don't move!'

Calypso took a step backwards.

'Madam! *I told you not to move!*'

She found herself staring directly into the eyes of a policeman, dilated, threatening. Crazy eyes. The policeman pushed hard up against her. He was breathing heavily, not actually looking at her; she was just a *thing* getting in his way. And that was when she saw Aslam. They were dragging him out of the house without his shoes. He was shivering violently and his feet were bare. Bare feet on a snow-covered London pavement? *What?* she thought.

The air was crystalline and the wind bitter. Aslam was wearing the green parrot-print shirt that Calypso had ironed earlier that morning. It was torn in two places and was no longer tucked into his trousers but hung over his waist, as though he'd been in a struggle of some sort. Calypso had bought him the shirt only last week.

They'd got Aslam with his hands up on the roof of the police car and they were searching him. He looked exactly like an actor in the television series Calypso liked to watch, or so she told me much later. She stared at him for a moment longer, stunned. Then she started shouting and waving her arms about. The snow was falling on her face and hair and she ignored it. Aslam was looking straight ahead and something seemed to be happening to Calypso's voice, weakening it. The policeman's armpit obscured her view. He was right up against her now, almost totally covering her eyes so she had to stand on tiptoe to see what was going on. He was a very big man; I mean, bulky, huge. Calypso could feel the heat from his body and hear the anger in his breathing. His uniform rubbed on her face and some metal object, a badge or a button, was digging into her cheek. She would remember this detail later when talking to me. At the time all she did was crane her neck in order to see a bit better. Aslam's hands were now behind his back. They'd handcuffed him and were shoving him into the car. It all happened very fast but at the very last minute, just before they got his head inside the car, he turned and saw Calypso.

And he smiled his beautiful smile.

He was trying to look as though he didn't care but *she* knew he was scared. She knew that look. Aslam started shouting but the police radios were crackling and Calypso couldn't hear what he was saying. Then there was a screech of tyres and the car drove off with wisps of snow skittering away from the wheels and in the livid cast of the light she realised she was screaming.

The policeman's arm relaxed and he appeared to forget about Calypso but the crowd seemed to grow bigger. She turned, caught sight of her cabbage again, lying in the gutter covered now in a shroud of snow, and without thinking picked it up. Then she ran towards the house, taking no notice of anyone. There were two officers blocking the doorway. She wanted to get inside as quickly as possible, to get away from the people staring at her. All the nosy neighbours were out gawping. Anything for a bit of drama. There was Mrs Brown and Mrs Putford, the two major gossips in the road. There was the woman called Clare who never spoke and whose children were scared of Calypso. Aslam, who couldn't care less about any of them, used to say they looked like washing powder.

Meaning they were pure white. Aslam used to say that in life appearance was all and you were never going to get over physical and cultural differences completely. Aslam, who at that moment was speeding away in a police car to God knows where.

By now even the Indian family was out on the pavement. Normally they pretty much kept themselves to themselves but who in their right mind was going to miss such a marvellous carry-on as this? Calypso wasn't taking any notice of anyone.

Let me in, she thought. What are you doing in my house? Why have you taken him away? What's going on?

The questions were only in her head. She didn't actually say a word. She was too busy trying to push past those policemen.

They let her in finally and then they closed the now broken door as far as they could. The electric lighting gave the place a saffron-yellow tinge. The snow had turned into sleet for the moment and was coming in fast. The bit of carpet nearest to the door was soaked in it. Outside, a policewoman was clearing the road and for a split second Calypso thought, oh yes, there's probably been a bomb scare but what has it got to do with Aslam? She was wet and shaking.

Slowly she began to take in what was happening. The house was in an absolute mess. The police had gone through to the lounge and the kitchen and on the way had behaved like wild buffaloes. Even the pictures on the walls had been smashed. Why? Calypso had no idea. Not then, not until much later. At the time she was only aware of rage: theirs, and hers. Later on she would understand that it wasn't rage but fear that had made them behave in this way. Fear, all of us would soon learn, is what controls everything that happens. Calypso hadn't had time to work any of this out yet, of course. All she was capable of was staring around in amazement. Eventually one of the officers told her *why* they had come into her house. They told her about the tip-off and how they had been watching the place for days, and they even went so far as to say they were sorry about the mess. Calypso just looked dazed, and in the end the policeman who'd been doing the talking tried asking questions in a less threatening way. Calypso was mute. In reality the policeman was only asking if she had someone who could be with her until her husband got back, but Calypso couldn't answer.

'Where have you taken him?' she asked eventually, meaning Aslam.

Because of course that was the only thing she wanted to know.

'He'll be at the police station, madam,' the policeman said. Then his radio crackled and he turned away to speak into it. Suddenly there were more people crowding into the house through the broken door and one of them, Calypso saw, was a policewoman and the other one was me, Hera.

The situation caught me head on. I, too, was soaking wet, in a hurry, and with troubles of my own. This was meant to be a quick visit so an earthquake wasn't what I had been anticipating. The policeman stared at me in surprise. This was a reaction I was used to. Calypso used to say it was because of how I looked.

'People don't expect to see a beautiful girl comg into this kind of house,' she would say, proudly. 'We Muslims are meant to be ugly under our burkas.'

Well, I didn't wear a burka and Calypso was entitled to her view. I'm her daughter so of course she thought I was beautiful. In any case, whatever the truth of the matter, I was used to being stared at.

So there I was coming in through that broken front door and the policewoman pounced on me and started questioning me. Who was I, what was my relationship to Aslam, where did I live, did I worship at the mosque, that sort of thing. Meanwhile, a police officer was taking the waste-paper baskets outside and, from the corner of my eye, I saw another policeman come down the stairs with a load of documents in his hands. It turned out there were passports, old diaries, instruction books for the heating system, naturalisation papers, our school and university certificates. You name it, they wanted it. Both men went straight out of the house without looking at us. It was just too much for Calypso: she started to collapse and Iris, walking in at that moment, caught her as she fell, and we moved her towards the settee. Iris was Calypso's friend … well, sort of. Calypso didn't really *do* friends!

Everyone was talking at once. Calypso's eyes were closed. She looked pale. I could see she was sweating in spite of the cold and, as there wasn't anything else I could do, I went into the kitchen to boil a kettle of water to make some sweet tea. To tell you the truth, I was feeling pretty scared myself and couldn't help wondering if really we should have been calling an ambulance. Still Iris seemed to know what she was doing so I just carried on making the tea.

By the time I had found some fresh mint in the fridge and steeped it in boiling water, Calypso was conscious again and it was thundering. The snow had begun to settle and the sky was so dark that the neighbours had been driven away. Only the reporters sheltering on the other side of the road were still watching our house like a group of bedraggled vultures. Suddenly I heard Calypso's voice. She was shouting, I mean really shouting, demanding a lawyer, demanding to know what had happened to Aslam. Okay, I thought, relieved; she's back to normal.

'No problem,' the policeman was saying. 'You get yourself a lawyer.'

But they were clearly not going to answer questions about Aslam. National Security was what they kept repeating. Calypso was beginning to go berserk. I shook my head.

What the hell should we do next? The police left soon after but the snow started up again, thickening as it fell. As they closed the door a blast of wind hit our faces sharply and I shivered. It had become suddenly much colder. For days everyone had been hoping against hope that the weather was easing up but clearly it was only getting worse. Shock does strange things and my skull felt like someone had cracked it open and the things inside were coming out in any old order. Meanwhile Calypso was beginning to sound like an old-fashioned piece of tape taken from a cassette recorder, the sort we used to undo with our little finger when we were children. High-pitched sounds were coming out of her mouth. I was talking to her but these sounds were her only reply. I tried to get her to drink the tea. Iris tried too but then she had to leave to pick up one of her kids so it was just me with Calypso now. Thankfully Uncle Lyle, our closest friend, appeared. He took in the wreckage, the broken sofa, Calypso huddled and shivering in a corner, and, Lyle being Lyle, immediately grasped the situation. He was very good like that. I don't know who'd told him but he'd come as fast as he could, he said. He sat down and I brought him a cup of mint tea, too. Then he turned to Calypso and started talking in a low voice. He spoke calmly and fast. I remember some of the things he said and not others.

Don't worry.

We have contacted Hektor.

He's on his way home.

We have contacted a lawyer who specialises in this sort of thing, too.

He is on the way to the police station to meet Aslam.

You must change your clothes because you are soaking wet.

Then we will go to the police station, too.

This mix-up will be sorted out, I promise.

Don't worry. They have mistaken Aslam for someone else, that's all.

It's this new security legislation that's the problem.

Now be strong and get ready.

I was listening very carefully. The tone of Lyle's voice bothered me. Once or twice he glanced in my direction in a warning sort of way and shook his head slightly. When he had finished speaking Calypso stood up. Then, with one swift movement, she threw her tea at the wall and turned and went upstairs without a word. I followed her.

Upstairs was in an even bigger mess. The yellowish light made the ransacked room look strangely beautiful. I stared at it intensely, as if looking at a familiar painting that, in my absence, had changed beyond recognition. They'd pulled the beds apart, the mattresses were thrown against the wall and the sheets were trailing on the floor along with the pillows. It was the same in Aslam's room, in all the bedrooms in fact. The cupboard on the landing had a hole in the door; there were books on the floor, papers everywhere. In the bathroom the light, perhaps because of the frosted-glass window, looked different again, softer, purer, contrasting with the violence done to it. The toilet seat had been partly ripped off, the

24

toilet brush thrown into the bath, and the medicine cabinet knocked from the wall so it swung wide open. All the things inside – the pills for Hektor's blood pressure, the plasters and the boxes of painkillers, the old bottles of cough medicine, the vitamin pills – had gone. Why would the police want them? Was someone ill at the police station? Calypso slammed the cupboard door hard and it crashed to the floor.

'Leave it!' I said sharply.

I took her arm and steered her into the bedroom.

'Here, wear this,' I said. 'Take your shoes off. And your socks; come on. Look at you, you're soaking wet. We should have got you out of these things earlier.'

Calypso was silent, her lips clamped together.

'Don't worry,' I said. 'Lyle is taking care of everything. Everything will be okay.'

I could see her struggling with some thought.

'Where's Hektor?' she asked, eventually.

Hektor is both my father and Calypso's husband. They, we have – how shall I put it? – a detached sort of relationship.

'He's on his way,' I said, although I couldn't be sure. 'He'll be here any minute now.'

She licked her upper lip and swallowed. I wondered if she was going up into the stratosphere. Hektor's temper is legendary but Calypso's is another matter. This mess was going to send them both straight into a war all of their own. Prayer and anger are a bad mix. Calypso finished getting dressed.

'You don't think …' she said, looking at me.

'No!' I said a little too quickly, a little too firmly. 'No, I don't. And neither should you. It's some sort of stupid mix-up. They will apologise, you'll see.'

'An apology won't be enough. Those people outside, that

woman … the Indian family and the shopkeeper across the road and …'

'Those people next door don't matter,' I said contemptuously. 'Who the hell are they? Nobodies.'

'It is okay for you,' Calypso said. 'You don't live here any more.'

'Stop it, for fuck's sake!'

She let the swear word go without flinching. After today, I guessed, there wouldn't be anything to make her flinch. I could see she was thinking something along these lines herself.

'Are you ready now?' I asked.

She glared at me. At least, I thought uneasily, she is trying to control her temper.

'I don't want you to be upset,' I said.

She was looking at me as if I had insulted her. And then we heard the front door open again and we both froze. But it was only Lyle coming back in with Hektor. They were talking in a low voice. Were they praying? I guessed so.

3.

The day the first powdery sprinkling of snow began to fall – six months after I met you – had been the day I realised I wanted to spend the rest of my life with you, Raphael. You, of course, had been interested only in the snow.

'Why?' I asked, laughing. 'I hate snow!'

In a way I understood that, for someone who had lived for most of his life on the driest part of the earth, snow might be exciting. You aren't the sort of person to get emotional about anything but you'd been watching the overcast sky for days and none had fallen. There were no stars, either, and you'd started complaining about this too. You've guessed right: I knew you were prone to bad moods. You stayed in bed, sleeping and refusing to see me. And when I rang you, even if you felt like answering the phone, you refused to say my name. Charming, huh?

Your cat and I were in the same category.

'This animal,' you grumbled, 'is demanding, like you.'

The cat would wake you each morning no matter how dull the light. For this reason, I knew you sometimes came close to hating the cat, as I'm sure you did me. Although for this very reason too, strangely, I knew you loved us both.

Not that you would have used the word *love*! God forbid.

That's too strong a word for your vocabulary. The mere suggestion of such a sentiment would have appalled you. Yet one evening, when you were a little drunk, you told me that the cat and I reminded you of someone you had once known.

'Who?' I asked eagerly.

You clammed up instantly and, disturbed, I sulked for a day.

On the morning after that first fall of snow, I went over to yours as usual. And, surprise, you were in a good mood.

'The Cretino jumped on me and woke me up,' you said, affectionately pointing at the cat. 'As usual.'

The Cretino, recognising your tone of voice, if not its latest name, purred encouragingly.

'Would you like a coffee?' you asked. You were fully dressed. 'Don't you think the garden looks magnificent? Come, let me show you!'

Naturally that first snow had transformed everything. I wasn't that interested but, having propelled me towards the window, you stared at it, mesmerised. With only a vague awareness of my presence, you stood gazing out for so long that the window steamed up with your breath and blurred the view.

The cat started yowling impatiently. You ignored it. I sipped my coffee. The garden had taken on a look of both lustre and desolation. A huge bird sailed past the window, its wings beating frantically as if it was having trouble staying airborne. The smaller black birds foraging for food scattered with frightened squawks but the peregrine, if it *was* a peregrine, vanished drunkenly out of sight. You remained lost in thought.

'Very occasionally,' you said, 'we used to see birds of prey in

28

the desert. They had the same markings as this one.'

I wasn't interested in birds.

'My wife didn't care for them,' you said, startling me.

I looked up. As you didn't often mention your dead wife, when you did – perhaps because the subject was always shrouded in mystery – I became interested. Of course I was jealous. I looked sharply at you.

'She felt they brought bad luck.'

You sighed.

'Your wife?' I asked deliberately, hoping you'd say her name.

No such luck, Raphael. You were too bloody-minded. You weren't about to divulge anything.

'My memory isn't what it used to be, you know,' you mumbled instead.

Oh, that's the game we're playing today, is it? I thought, uneasily.

'It's many years since I left that place,' you added. 'I've tried to wash the dirt off but …'

The cat scratched politely at the door and I let it out. The hot-water pipes were making a noise.

A bit later on, looking a little shamefaced, you admitted you'd been out in your observatory.

'But the place is freezing,' I said.

You shrugged. You'd turned on the heating, hadn't you, and switched on the various motors? So what was the problem?

'But it will take days to warm up with that heater of yours. Raphael, you'll get ill again! I told you not to go out.'

'I wore my gloves,' you muttered, furiously. 'And my coat and two scarves. What more d'you want?'

I stared at you in dismay.

'I *told you* to stay indoors.'

29

'*Told me? I do as I please, miss.*'

Let me remind you of the sequence of events. You, Raphael, had had a bad dose of flu, so bad in fact that I'd become alarmed. Calypso had once been very ill with pneumonia. It had been touch and go as to whether she went to hospital. We'd all been worried. So I knew about chests.

'Once you weaken your lungs,' I told you, 'death follows.'

'Good!' you said. 'What do I care?'

Ignoring you, and remembering what had happened to Calypso, I'd insisted on taking you to the emergency clinic.

'Just to be on the safe side.'

Raphael, you hadn't behaved too well at the time.

'I've never been on the safe side,' you'd bellowed.

Can you believe it? *Everyone* in the waiting room had stared at us. You could be a nightmare when you wanted to.

'My goodness,' the doctor, also a woman, had remarked, 'you've got a helluva voice for such a sick person!'

The doctor and you had glared at each other and I'd tried not to laugh. Silly old fool! The doctor, assuming you were my difficult father, had taken my side, praising my patience. This naturally drove you crazy. The doctor told you off. Then she gave you some antibiotics (which you later threw away after taking only two) and told you to wrap up warmly. You grunted, avoiding my eye, but as a compromise took your scarf from your pocket and wound it around your neck with a sour look. Honestly, why did I bother? I was nineteen. You, Raphael, were old enough to *be* my father!

On the bus going back we hadn't spoken. You had sat hunched morosely in your seat, and I looked out of the window. I think you sensed I was upset but this made you even more stubborn, so that you sat with a defiant expression on your face even though you couldn't stop coughing. Raphael, you didn't care that you were being a shit. And when I paid you a visit the next day we'd had a row.

'Why don't you put the central heating on?' I'd asked. 'This stove of yours is pretty disgusting.'

You ignored me.

'I've got a spare fan heater, if you'd prefer?' I'd said.

You didn't bother to answer.

'It's stupid to keep using a smelly stove. You're living in the twenty-first century for heaven's sake. In the middle of London.'

Your only answer was to suck your cheeks in and turn your back on me.

You looked as stubborn as your cat.

'You'll burn your house down one of these days.'

You looked as if you wanted to hit me.

'Leave me alone. Are you some sort of spy? Or a member of the secret police?'

'Stop being such a nasty bugger,' I shouted.

'If you don't like it then go away.'

'I will if that's what you want, old man, but I don't think it is.'

'You'll be a case by the time you're forty, you know. I'm already feeling sorry for your future husband, God protect him!'

'Right,' I said, grabbing my coat and my sketchbook. 'That's it! I'm bloody going. Stay in your stupid house feeling sorry for yourself. Just because your wife has died doesn't mean you have to take it out on me. Millions of people have wives that die. But you …' I'd paused for breath, 'you just feel sorry for yourself. See if I care!'

There, I'd said it. The words couldn't be taken back. I swallowed.

You fell silent. I glanced fearfully at you, biting my lip. You looked a bit crushed. We stood glaring at each other, not knowing what to do next.

'Have some sage tea,' you said finally.

It had been our first row.

Two weeks passed and then I brought some food: a braised quail with something called tamar hindi. You had no idea what this was or even where I'd got the quail. I had also brought bread, some onions and cardamom rice fried in a little oil and sprinkled with paprika. Seeing your look of surprise, I must have blushed. You knew I didn't have much money, didn't you, Raphael?

'Ah,' you said triumphantly. 'You've pinched this from your mother's house, haven't you?'

Well, it was true.

'So you're a thief too!' you said but you wolfed the food down all right. And then you smiled at me and said a bit gruffly that you were sorry. For arguing so much, I suppose. This was a big step forward.

Afterwards I washed up the mess in the sink, wiped the oilskin tablecloth, and made a pot of tea. I wasn't planning on drawing you that day. The truth was you looked a bit weak and I was secretly still a little worried about you.

'You need to eat nourishing food,' I said. 'Dried fish and chilli every day isn't much good when you've been ill. You need something warming.'

I'd had my back to you and so didn't see the warning look on your face. The next moment you forgot all about your apology and started behaving badly again. Honestly, you were such a nightmare!

'You can't blame me,' you shouted. 'It's my way of life. Why shouldn't I live it?'

'Have you been taking your antibiotics?' I asked.

'I've finished them,' you bellowed.

You were lying, of course.

'So what's this, then?' I asked, showing you the packet in the bin.

'Mind your own business.'

But when I gave you a glass of water you swallowed a tablet, albeit reluctantly.

'And keep away from your shed for a bit?' I said.

'I told you not to call it a *shed* ...'

'Why haven't you put the heating on like I told you?'

'Don't push me,' you muttered, scowling. 'I may be old but I've still a little fight left.'

It was like dealing with a small child. I sighed, pointedly. Why I was so drawn to you, Raphael, was a mystery.

My painting of you was progressing nicely; the drawings I was making were good, and my tutor was full of praise. But, although good portraiture was all about understanding character, I knew very little about yours. Most of what you told me was rather fragmentary. I sensed that you'd had some sort of trauma over your wife's death but, when I asked you if she'd died in an accident or through illness, you'd glared at me, looking so furious that I'd shivered and shut up. But then you suddenly volunteered the information that once your life had been filled with noise!

'*Noise?*' I asked, astonished by such an odd remark.

You nodded. Yes.

'What sorts of noise?'

Motorbikes.

Car horns.

Voices.

The wind rustling in the trees.

The telephone ringing.

And voices everywhere. Even, after some years, unbelievably, the sound of singing.

The words brought a slow wetness around your eyes, I noticed, and I was consumed by tenderness.

And after the snow came I sensed you were a little happier. You'd become a bit more talkative, too.

'If the clouds clear there will be stars,' you'd said.

And then, your good mood restored, you went on to tell me about the stars. Your voice had had an unbearable lightness to it that made me feel excluded. Suddenly I felt sad. Was it a premonition of what was to come?

4.

G uess what Hektor said when he walked in.
'I thought it had stopped but it's bloody snowing,
again!'

Can you believe it? With the front door off its hinges, with
Aslam in a police station, being held for God knows what
crime, with the house ransacked and Calypso practically
hyperventilating, Hektor was preoccupied with the weather.
I wanted to hit him and, if I hadn't stopped her, Calypso
might have done the job for us both. Calypso and Hektor had
a weird relationship which I didn't altogether understand. In
my opinion this had been one of Aslam's main problems.
Mine too.

In the car, on the way to the police station, Hektor sat in
the front and Lyle drove. We were silent. The air had turned
a sharp metallic blue and the snow had begun to settle. It
formed a thin crust on the pavements and, because of the
encroaching darkness and the configuration of the clouds,
you could almost imagine there were mountains in the
distance. A plane sped overhead. An unusual sound these
days, for with the shortage of fuel only those with real money
could afford air travel. I wondered what it would be like to
fly over the white counties, to see from above the fields and

towns, the blocked motorways of England. I thought of the geography of snow and how a girl the police had recently found, not much older than me, had been murdered and left like detritus, naked in a wood. Snow was good for hiding things, I thought. I shivered.

To distract myself with pleasant thoughts I did what I used to do as a child. I began imagining the stories Calypso used to tell me. Of the street vendors with their charcoal burners and the smell of roasting coffee and spice that saturated the air. I had always loved Calypso's stories of her past in the Middle East. I wanted her world to be mine too. Although I had rejected most things that were taught to us in our community, still, I was proud to be an Arab girl.

'Being a Muslim isn't all about prayers and headscarves,' I used to argue hotly.

Before the war came to her country, Calypso used to say, the students had been hopeful. They believed in their youth and that they could change all those things their elders had ruined. In those times of peace, before every joyous thing was restricted, there used to be music and feast days.

'The nights were without fear,' Calypso would say. 'We had the most enormous stars imaginable.'

She had been ten when the war started brewing. Life as she knew it was on the way out.

We were silent in the back of the car, each thinking our own fragmented thoughts. Suddenly, Hektor turned sharply to look at us.

'Here,' he said in what was a conciliatory tone for him, 'pray, will you!'

And he threw a string of beads at me. They fell behind his seat and Calypso picked them up. The car stopped at a traffic light.

'Not long now,' I mouthed, squeezing Calypso's hand.

Her hands were cold. Praying would not warm them.

My mother jerked her head towards Hektor's back and pulled a face. He was praying loudly. In spite of the seriousness of the moment, perhaps *because* of it, I wanted to laugh. Hysteria was attempting to burst through my fear. But let me put the record straight. Hektor wasn't such a bad man. Coming from a culture where such things were permissible, he didn't beat his wife. And he did get her out of a different kind of hell, didn't he, bringing her to Britain, providing for her as best he could? These days he no longer had the will to control my mother. She was too strong, too wild for him now. I'm sure he must have wondered who on earth he had married. Calypso continued to do as she pleased. Hektor merely grumbled about the bad wife that she was. Yet I had this curious feeling that, in his uninformed way, he was a little proud of her because, let's face it, she was unlike any other woman in their community. She was not afraid to speak her mind. The only thing I would say that still upset her was the business of losing the chance of an education.

She was singing softly under her breath now. Something about mothers having their careers cut out for them when the child in the womb stirs. It was obvious she was trying to be positive about Aslam. The snow was falling in a transparent curtain, muffling our despair in its fall. It was beginning to obscure the road signs and make the street lights appear harsh above us as a cold blueness from a passing ambulance lit up our faces. The windscreen wipers were working furiously and Lyle, unusually for him, was swearing under his breath. The rest of us remained silent.

'The lawyer should already be there,' Lyle said.

He glanced at Calypso in the mirror but Calypso looked away. All around us the snow continued to fall, thick and heavy and white. The speed with which it fell added to the strange lethargy that was descending on us. We crossed the snaking bone of the river. Had it not been for the bridge no one would have known there was water underneath.

'He didn't have a sweater,' Calypso said, speaking with a dangerous casualness.

Lyle was giving her worried glances in the mirror.

'It's okay,' I said. 'I picked one up when I went into his room.'

Lyle shook his head very slightly and Calypso nodded. They had always been this way together, communicating wordlessly.

'Being cold is the least of his troubles,' Hektor said, irritated by something he was only dimly aware of.

'Hektor,' Lyle said. 'Now's not the time.'

'Yes,' Calypso agreed. 'Where were you when he needed *your* guidance?'

'I tried to bring him up to be a worthwhile person. Someone who knew right from wrong.'

'Since when did praying teach a person right from wrong? That's like thinking that if you learn the times-tables off by heart it will make you a mathematician.'

'Shut your mouth, woman,' Hektor said. 'Or I'll wash it out with disinfectant!'

He spoke without heat. Once again, Lyle looked at Calypso through his mirror.

'How's he going to do that?' Calypso asked in her husky, sing-song voice. 'Has he brought disinfectant with him in the car?'

I pressed my lips together, laughter bubbling up in my throat again. Lyle was trying to keep a straight face, too.

'Perhaps my husband will ask those nice policemen at the police station, with his nice Leeds accent, if he could take me to the bathroom to wash my mouth?' Calypso said.

I could feel my shoulders shake.

'Lyle,' she said, her voice changing abruptly. 'D'you remember the sound the dead reeds made in winter? Do you remember how it snowed, there?'

Lyle had his eyes on the road now. 'It wasn't like this,' he said uneasily, pointing ahead. 'This is weird.'

The snow was a feather-fall, a sigh descending with deceptively sweet speed. Hektor was giving us a magnificent display of prayers, pointedly ignoring them both.

'My grandmother used to make a kind of mint tea in those days out of the plants dried from the summer. D'you remember, Lyle?'

Lyle nodded. 'I haven't tasted anything like it anywhere else in the world.'

'How many places in the world have you been to, then?' Hektor asked.

'She used to say the wild mint from the marshes was different from the cultivated variety,' Calypso said, raising her voice.

Any minute now, I thought, someone is going to explode.

'D'you remember, Lyle,' Calypso asked insistently, 'the silvery-white smoke from the buffalo dung?'

Why was she deliberately antagonising Hektor?

'Yes,' Lyle said.

Calypso took a deep breath and turned to me.

'In the summer,' she continued, 'we used to eat the fish

we caught from the lagoon. My grandfather and my cousins would spike them with their three-pronged spears. Didn't they, Lyle?'

Oh God, she's spoiling for a fight, I thought nervously.

'Yes,' Lyle said, his voice even.

'They would roast the fish over an open fire, Hera, and serve them together with great circles of flat bread. The bread was very fresh, not like the stuff you get here.'

I stared at my hands. Don't include me in these games, I thought.

'Whenever we visited my grandparents, we would bring them date treacle from the city to eat with their buffalo curd.'

The car sped along the silent streets and Hektor leaned towards Lyle. He said something in a low voice and the two of them began talking softly together.

'What are you saying?' Calypso asked, leaning forward.

'Don't worry,' Hektor said quickly. 'Leave it to us.'

This is how we sorted things out in our family. The women stayed silent and left it to the men. And when the men ruined everything we still said nothing. There was something growing large in my chest. I could feel it expanding and spreading inside the car.

'Aslam handcuffed in a police station?' Calypso said. 'Surrounded by men who will do him harm? What are you saying?'

I put my hand on her arm to restrain her. I, too, could not stop thinking of Aslam, alone with a series of accusations that might or might not be true. Without a lawyer.

'Hold on,' Lyle said calmly. 'You're going far too fast! Wait and see. I am confident.'

'I'm certain it's a mistake,' I agreed, not certain at all. 'Think

40

of the marshes, Calypso. Go there in your mind.'

'Wait,' Lyle said, looking into the mirror.

His words sounded like a caress. A pain as sharp as glass shot through me and I thought of you, Raphael.

Hektor was still praying. His main contribution to life, I thought dully, was to pray and command us to do the same. Then Lyle turned off the main road and the police station loomed ahead. It was a square container of a building. A place of concrete indifference. All four of us were instantly silent again. We stared. I shivered. Then I opened the door and stepped out onto a clean, thickening layer of untrodden snow.

5.

The day I first set eyes on you, Raphael, the weather had been foul. We had had an astonishingly long and depressing winter with heavy rains every single day. The city that had once been so sparkling and full of life, with its neon theatres, its early-evening crowded bars, its street-food stalls, was now in a state of dour lethargy, awful to see. The government had become weak and was fragmenting. The only way we got to change things was by protest and petitions, although even that didn't often work. Things were falling apart. I was in my second year at the art school and had been late handing in a project to my tutor. I'd asked for an extension of another week but I was stuck, feeling uninspired. Perhaps the awfulness of the weather was the reason. Perhaps it was because I'd had another row with Hektor, who was urging me to meet the son of some idiot now praying at our mosque. I was sick of Hektor and his unsubtle ways. I'd rung Aslam up, hoping for his support, but my brother had surprised me by suggesting I meet the boy Hektor had in mind.

'*What?*' I screamed. 'Are you crazy or something?'

'Don't be so closed, Hera,' he said. 'At least meet the guy. He might be an okay sort of Muslim, you never know.'

'What are you talking about?' I snapped. 'Since when did

you become a bloody practising Muslim?'

'I'm just telling you not to be so mulish,' Aslam had said.

Hurt and surprised, I had a huge row with him. After I cut him off, I picked up my sketchbook, put my coat on, and went out to the small café across the road from my tiny room. The rain was now sleet.

You were at the counter, Raphael, paying for something or other, and your face was turned towards the door when I walked in. I was cursing under my breath. For a moment our eyes met. Bloody corny, huh? And I bet you can't even remember the moment. Well, it's what happened anyway. There was a fraction of a second's pause; a nanosecond of time and also an eternity. It pulled me up sharply. I felt the earth spin. D'you know you had quite simply the most beautiful face I'd ever seen, a little crinkled around the eyes and with such a sad expression in them. Instantly I wanted to draw you. But you left without a backward glance and I sat down with a cup of coffee. I was trembling. That was all that happened that day. The next afternoon I went back to the café and had another coffee, hoping you'd be there. But there was no sign of you. I stayed there for so long that the owner came across and asked me if there was anything else I wanted.

'No,' I said. 'But I am looking for that man in the camel-coloured coat.'

Of course, the café owner didn't know who I was talking about but he asked the waitress, who nodded. She knew who I meant.

'He often comes in on a Thursday.'

It was only Tuesday. Two whole days to wait. And what if this gorgeous man didn't come in again, ever? I decided to come in every day on the off-chance you changed your habits.

I skipped college and sat drawing over endless cups of coffee. Bet you didn't know that! The light was bad but I continued to sit stubbornly, drawing everything that existed in the café. In two days I filled a whole notebook. From time to time the owner would come over and look at my sketches in amazement. I think he thought it pretty cool having a student drawing in his café. But, Raphael, you did not come and I was filled with an unaccountable despair. It was as though I had discovered a piece of myself, only to have it vanish into thin air. It was the strangest sensation of *déjà vu* that I had ever experienced. And it made me edgy and afraid. Am I expressing myself clearly enough? Is it possible to use mere words to describe this almost electrical fusion that took place? In the end I spent three weeks in the café before I saw you again. And on *that* ink-dark, icy night the world suddenly filled up with stars.

With your arrival, miraculously, the rain stopped for the first time in seven months and the temperature soared to twenty-two. It's true! Spring and summer rolled into one with the birds waking up. This situation would last for a month only, during which time I managed to talk to you, find out your name was Raphael and persuade you – the hardest part of all – to allow me to paint you. Good God! You were impossibly prickly. I remember the moment your outright hostility surfaced. Painting was something you knew very little about and I suppose I took you by surprise. To start with you told me nothing except your name, your address and what time I was to arrive for the sitting. The rest was private information.

'One hour,' you said sourly. 'No more. You can do your drawing and leave. Understood?'

I should have sensed trouble but of course I didn't. Although I didn't realise it I was already smitten.

It was the waitress who told me about the observatory you had built at the back of your house, how you would work in it late into the night. Watching the stars. You, Raphael, told me nothing. You would have been mortified had you known they'd talked about you in this way.

'He'll build a spaceship next,' the café owner said jokingly. 'And hopefully take us all away from this dying planet.'

The man meant no harm. I even think he liked you, Raphael.

That had been months ago. Quite a lot had happened between us since then, although ironically nothing physical and nothing too personal on your part. Yes, I was falling in love. But, and this is a big but, our relationship was progressing so incredibly slowly that I was going mad. You were a cool number. You let me draw you (it was going okay and in fact my tutor thought the drawings were amazing) but you showed no interest whatsoever in the drawings and you made it very clear from the start you wanted no friendship. The other rule, which was mega-ridiculous, was that I should paint you with the stars of the universe as a backdrop. Unbelievable!

'I am a serious artist,' I shouted. 'I can't paint such a stupid background. Have you no sensibilities?'

I sounded like Calypso. You folded your lips together, ready to do battle.

'The universe is serious,' was all you said.

Stubborn old goat. In the end I gave in. I would simply have to make two paintings, I decided.

*

I learnt three things about you before I realised I was falling in love.

Your wife was dead.

You hated sunlight.

And you didn't like to be touched.

I still had no idea how old you were. But I didn't care. I just wanted to sleep with you.

6.

As we entered the police station I noticed how dark it had become, like an oil painting that had been allowed to get dirty. Suddenly I was afraid. No good will come of this, I thought, with a shiver. Three hours had passed since Aslam had been taken. A lot can happen in that time if you are unrepresented and in custody. Any fool knows that. I looked nervously at Calypso. She appeared to be in a trance. This frightened me more than if she had been screaming because screaming is always what I expected from my mother. The lawyer that Lyle had contacted was waiting for us. He had pale skin and red hair. I knew my mother would be thinking this was a bad sign. I also knew that if Lyle was turning to a white person for help it meant things were serious. I didn't want to think of the implications.

'It would appear the police think your son is a *fanboy*,' the lawyer said. His eyes were very slightly hooded.

This was the first time I had heard the word. He began explaining what this meant with a slightly apologetic air. By the time he'd finished speaking Hektor was spluttering with rage.

'What's he talking about?' he asked, turning to Lyle. 'I want to see my son.'

The policeman on the desk, who'd been eyeing us slyly, stood up now and Hektor turned to him.

'What are you accusing my son of?' he bellowed.

'I'm not accusing him, sir,' the policeman said calmly. There was an unmistakable edge to his voice. 'He's merely been taken in for questioning.'

We were all talking at once. Suddenly Hektor moved towards the policeman but Lyle was quicker. He grabbed him by the sleeve.

'Obeying orders, are you?' Hektor asked nastily, trying to shake Lyle off at the same time.

'Hektor,' Lyle said wearily.

The policeman gazed at a point just above their heads. Then, slowly, he lowered his eyes until he met Hektor's. I thought he was going to swat my father. A door opened and another man in plain clothes came out. Immediately the lawyer, whose name I can't remember, went up to him. There was a hurried discussion after which we were ushered into an interview room. They weren't going to let me in but at the last minute they did, presumably because they thought I might know something of importance. Which of course I didn't. What Aslam got up to wasn't my business. Although I doubted he was into the sort of stuff they were accusing him of, still, I wasn't my brother's keeper. Fanboys, by the way, are Desert Death Squad supporters and possible facilitators for the recruitment process. I wanted to laugh out loud. Anyone who knew Aslam wouldn't believe him capable of being part of such things. Aslam is a pacifist; he hates the Death Squads. Obviously the police were just panicking. Or looking for a scapegoat, which was scary in a different way. Hektor's eyes were filled with rage. He hated the police at the best of times and I could see he wasn't going to keep silent.

The combination of his anger and these two police officers was a lethal cocktail. I swallowed.

'So I was right, then,' he said, changing tack, 'he's brought it on himself and caused his mother and me all this distress.'

Nice one, Hektor.

'Shut up,' Calypso said.

There was a tricky silence. I don't believe I've ever heard Calypso speak so rudely to Hektor in this way. In public, too. I felt like ducking. But before he could react, both Lyle and the lawyer were asking for more information. When could they see their client? Where was he being held? What *exactly* was the charge? Had he in fact been charged at all because, if not, he could not be held for too long. Calypso stood up. She looked scary, her hair poking out from under her scarf. And then the door opened and another police officer came in, holding out a file. We were each required to make a statement and, in my case, I was expected to fill out a questionnaire. I stared at the clipped pieces of paper. The questions were completely idiotic, things like how much did I trust the police and whether I believed my religion was the correct one. I pushed the questionnaire back towards the officer. It was disgusting! There was no way I could answer it.

'I don't believe in any God,' I said. 'And what's it to do with my brother?'

The policeman looked at me. It was the first time I had spoken and clearly I had startled him. Aslam called this sort of stuff the *preconception of the masses*. I could see what he meant.

'Look, miss,' the policeman said, 'I don't want to upset you but this is routine procedure. If you help us everything will be a lot quicker for you. Just fill in the form. Please?'

He spoke quietly; he was almost smiling at me, can you believe? I am not what you expect, I thought. Neither am I, his eyes pleaded. He was about my age. Was I meant to feel sorry for him?

'Yes,' Hektor said. 'Fill it in, quickly now. And don't write rubbish about no God, either.'

'Oh, shut up,' I said.

Calypso gave a short laugh. The officer was looking at Hektor with some distaste. I filled in the form as quickly as I could, writing N/A in answer to nearly all of the questions. Then I pushed it back across the table.

'Your age?' he asked. 'You haven't filled it in.'

'Nineteen,' I said.

'Where d'you work?'

'I don't.'

'She's at bloody art school,' Hektor bellowed.

And he glared at me again.

'Why don't you write that down, idiot girl?' he asked.

I didn't bother to reply. Idiot yourself, I thought, returning the policeman's stare. He was the first to lower his eyes.

And after all that, finally, they told us Aslam had been moved and we couldn't see him.

'Where to?' the lawyer asked.

'I'm afraid I can't say …'

'What the hell d'you mean?' Hektor demanded. 'I'm going to ring up the newspapers …'

'Hektor,' Lyle said.

'Hektor,' Calypso said.

I could see she could have said more but was restraining herself. The windows were high. It was impossible to see what was going on outside.

'You can't deny me information about my son,' Hektor was saying. 'We are law-abiding citizens; you cannot hold him for no reason, you cannot …'

The officer kept on repeating that Aslam was perfectly safe, that by law they had the right to question him for another twelve hours and that it was important for them to ascertain if he was part of a cell. A *cell*? Stunned, we couldn't think of anything to say.

I saw the lawyer hesitate.

'Well, it's only a few more hours,' he said easily.

'Come back in the morning,' we were told. 'We'll have a bit more information for you.'

A second later, we found ourselves outside. How could they do this to us? It was unbelievably inhuman.

Although he hadn't said much, Lyle was as angry as we were. He and the lawyer stood a little way apart. I could see they were disagreeing about something but I couldn't quite catch what it was.

'I'm afraid they *can*,' the lawyer kept insisting. 'If it's a matter of national security they can do almost anything.'

He looked towards Calypso nervously. No doubt he had never met anyone like her before. She was standing in the falling snow without moving. I wasn't sure how much she'd taken in, but I alone knew what she was feeling. I could feel the cold seeping in through my trainers. It was spreading from my feet upwards, slowly, numbingly. I put my arm around my distraught mother but she did not move. Neither of us said anything. Then, at last, Lyle and the lawyer came to a decision. They told us they were going back in to talk to the police officer. It just didn't seem right that we had so little information. It was difficult to know what the lawyer was really thinking. He appeared indifferent and I wondered if he was any good. Perhaps Lyle had made a mistake by hiring him because the man certainly didn't look too worried. As if he read my thoughts, Lyle gave me a warning look. My job was obviously to keep an eye on both my parents, make sure they stayed calm.

One thing both the lawyer and Lyle agreed on was that Hektor should stay out of it for the moment.

'Why?' he asked. 'Why can't I come in with you?'

But the other two had hurried off.

'Dad,' I said.

I stopped. What could I say, really? That the clothes he was wearing didn't actually help the situation? Hektor's white shift was soaked and he was shivering. Appearance was all, I thought bitterly.

'They think I'm a fool,' he said.

He sounded defeated. So the three of us waited in the car park for what seemed like ages. I stood with my trainers buried in snow. Calypso, too, was freezing.

'Well,' she said, eventually, 'he has red hair. What d'you expect?'

I opened my mouth to say something to them both about the inappropriate way they were behaving, but their faces looked so pinched and they were so clearly frightened that I didn't have the heart to upset them further. In that moment and with no warning I saw them as they really were, their powerlessness and their defeat. They had been in the West for so long, had raised a family, lived and worked in this place yet they were no more integrated than if they'd arrived yesterday. Nomads in every sense of the word, they belonged nowhere. Suddenly, in the face of their love for Aslam, I felt overcome by sorrow. I could not speak.

And all the while, the city continued to become embalmed in the whiteness, huge flakes of snow swirling and tumbling endlessly through the rising wind. It filled our mouths and our noses. It took our breath away. Very soon others would be casualties of what was happening.

Hektor stared woodenly ahead. He had taken out his beads and was turning them restlessly.

'We are nobodies,' he mumbled. 'We count for nothing.'

'What are you talking about,' Calypso said, 'we have *never* counted for anything.'

She spread her hands up towards the falling snow.

'When have the ordinary people mattered? In what country? In what culture?'

Hektor looked away.

'Time you faced the truth, old man,' she continued. 'We are brought up to believe we have an identity but the truth is we are all the same. We are drones. You, me, the children, everyone.'

The front door of the police station opened and Lyle appeared.

'Why don't you sit in the car?' he suggested, offering Hektor the keys. 'I'll be back in a minute.'

'What's happening?' Hektor asked but Lyle had gone in again.

In the car, with the heater blowing hard and snow covering the windscreen, all three of us sat in the back seat. Our morose patience reminded me of the way cattle huddled together in the winter fields. It was the closest we had been in years. In the silence I could hear my watch ticking. Ten minutes passed and then another ten.

53

'I'm going in,' Calypso said at last.

'Don't be a fool,' Hektor snapped. 'You're a woman. I'll go.'

'I'm his mother,' Calypso said.

She sounded uncertain.

The gap between us was opening up once more. In the chasm I saw my parents' fear stretched out darkly against the whitening landscape outside. Their faces were troubled against the snow, their hands small and restless. With a rush of fierce love, I wanted to protect them both. A piece of cloth poked out from underneath Calypso's shabby coat.

It was blue like the eyes we had inherited from her.

It symbolised all that she no longer had, all that she still might lose. I wrenched open the car door.

'Stay here,' I said. 'I'll find them.'

And I ran out into the relentless cold before they could stop me.

The moment I walked through the door, the lights failed and we were plunged abruptly into darkness. This was followed by an electronic whine that faded into silence. A male voice cursed softly and almost immediately a torch was switched on.

'Power cut,' the voice said.

I heard Lyle cough.

'Go back to the car, Hera,' he said, quietly.

Another torch was switched on. I saw the lawyer and Lyle illuminated in it like figures in a Georges de La Tour picture. All we need are some cards, I thought, irrelevantly. And then I saw a policeman bring in a few candles. We spoke all together.

'Sorry about this,' the policeman said. 'It's never happened before.' He pulled a face. 'This weather! Now where was I …'

'Aslam …' I began.

'Yes, miss,' he said. 'That's what I've been telling your uncle and your lawyer. I do understand how difficult this must be for you.'

In the unexpected darkness his voice had softened. For a split second I felt we might just be a man and a woman meeting for the first time; in a café, without fear or religious prejudice. I felt rather than saw him stare at me. But the image of my brother stood between us.

'Where *is* he?'

'Hera,' Lyle said warningly.

'As I said, he's been taken to a central office for interrogation. It's just routine. Nothing to worry about.'

And then, as if on cue, the lights came on again.

So we could not visit Aslam but, yes, he would be able to contact his lawyer *after* the interview. As to his return, well, the policeman shrugged, it wasn't up to him, the matter was out of his hands now.

'Okay,' the lawyer said. 'Here's my card. And can you tell him to ring me as soon as his interview is over? At any time, day or night?'

'Yes,' the policeman said, and he politely took the card, turning it over and over in his hand.

Why did I have the feeling that he'd toss it into the waste-paper basket the minute our backs were turned? He walked towards the door and held it open. The interview was over.

'You'll hear from him soon, I'm sure,' he said.

And again he looked at me and smiled very slightly. He wore a gold band on his ring finger. I tried to imagine what he might have been like when he was off duty, smiling at his wife, making love to her, playing with his children. A good man, a man known to be kind, respected in his community. The sort of man who could be relied upon.

'Goodbye, miss,' he said and the door swung shut.

We walked back to the car. The lawyer slipped into the front passenger seat. I went in the back and saw that Hektor, *Hektor*, was crying.

'They're questioning him still,' Lyle said. 'That's all they would say.'

'Where?' Calypso asked. 'Why?' Her voice was harsh as a crow's.

'They say he was plotting to commit an act of terrorism.'

Hektor gave a great wail.

'Shut up, old man,' Calypso screamed.

'Oh my God! What evidence do they have?'

'What are you going to do about it?' I demanded.

'I want to see Aslam,' Calypso said. She sounded like a child.

'I'm taking you all home,' Lyle said. 'And then I'm going back to the office. We'll sort it out – you mustn't worry. We really will. I'll find out where he is, I promise.'

'I'm coming with you,' Hektor said, angry again.

Lyle shook his head. 'No, Hektor. This has to be done by us in the proper way.'

'He's *my* responsibility,' Hektor bellowed.

'You can't come,' Lyle said firmly.

'He's right,' I said. 'You'll just make everything worse. You both will.'

Hektor was shouting. 'Why? Why?'

'Listen, Hektor ...' Lyle said.

He hesitated, then turned the engine on and swept the snow off the windscreen in two wide arcs. The snow made a soft thudding noise but, even as the windscreen cleared, more fell on it.

'Listen to me. Look at what you are wearing! Look how you lose your temper, listen to the way you shout, look at your bloody beads … Why carry them around so openly … as if you are an extremist … No, stop a moment …' He raised his hand before Hektor could protest. 'There is nothing *wrong* with how you dress or how you pray or how you worry, but in these circumstances, with this kind of suspicion and fear floating around Aslam, it's best you keep out of sight. Let me deal with it, okay?'

'So, you are ashamed of me.'

'Oh God, Hektor,' Lyle said, under his breath.

'No, Hektor,' the lawyer told him. 'Not shame, not suspicion, just common sense. Keep out of sight, okay? Let us deal with this. We will get your boy back, I promise.'

There was a pause. The windscreen was covered in snow again. It was a complete whiteout in every sense of the word.

'Right,' Lyle said, glancing at me in the mirror. 'Let's go.'

I remembered then, we had forgotten to give the police Aslam's sweater.

'Don't worry,' Lyle said. 'Don't worry, don't worry, I'll take it with me.'

'He's a good boy,' Calypso said to no one in particular in an odd sort of voice.

We turned and looked at her. She is breaking up, I thought.

'Good or bad,' Lyle said, shaking his head. 'Enemies of Britain or their allies. It's a stupid simplistic argument!'

But had he been saying things to incite violence?

'Lyle,' Calypso asked. 'Is he going to be all right? Really all right?'

Lyle nodded but he wouldn't look at her.

'My son has done nothing wrong unless thinking is wrong,' Calypso said.

'They are rounding up more young people,' the lawyer said, reluctantly. 'His associates.'

Associates?

'He's a student. Who are these associates?'

'Other fanboys,' Lyle said, his voice flat.

The lawyer said nothing more. He's being careful, I thought. He doesn't want to make any mistake. *He knows more than he's saying.*

'Fanboy? Fanboy?' Calypso said.

Everyone ignored her.

'Fanboys,' she said again and I wanted to hit her.

Hektor was crying again.

More snow thudded on the roof of the car. The world was being obliterated by it. It felt as though we were living in a fairy tale gone terribly wrong.

'They use internet chatrooms as they feel safer this way. They have multiple pseudonyms in order not to be identified.'

'And are you saying my son does this?' Calypso asked.

'It's your fault,' Hektor shouted in sudden fury, tears all gone, pointing his finger at me. 'You've got something to do with this.'

Me? Leave me out of this, *please.*

'As for you,' he continued, turning on Calypso, 'you've always encouraged him to be different. *You've* done this, *you've* ruined all our lives, the business I've built up over so many years, my …'

His face had turned a strange shade of brown; his white hair was uncombed and greasy underneath the cap. I could see dandruff on his jacket. He was fingering his beads furiously.

'Dad,' I said.

Calypso wasn't even looking at him; it was as if he didn't exist.

'You are talking like a shit,' she said quietly in Arabic.

And now there was a dangerous edge to her voice.

'Enough,' Lyle said. 'For God's sake, enough of this senseless fighting. Let's stick together, just get through this night and in the morning we *will* get our answers.'

We dropped the lawyer at his office. He promised to phone Lyle in an hour's time. I watched as he hurried off, his smart overcoat a dark smudge against the white landscape, his receding figure uncomplicated and simply drawn. The snow fell in broken lines, disjointedly, as we drove through it slowly. The soft richness of it was like a mink stole. It draped itself over the city with languid indifference while the street lights twinkled like small jewels on the ground. Yes, it was breathtakingly lovely to look at but there was no comfort in it. And although there *was* a kind of enchantment it did not touch me. Something was terribly wrong. Underneath the pretty whiteness of our city lurked a darker story we none of us could as yet understand. But just as in the stories Calypso used to tell me as a child, those old tales of injustice enacted elsewhere, in places that no longer existed, something similar was approaching. Aslam had once said that nothing happens in isolation. The past, my brother believed, remained dormant. It refuses to be erased.

'All small wars will eventually link up,' he once had told me. 'And we will be caught up in them, all over again, you'll see.'

During his late-night arguments with Calypso and me,

when we were growing up, he used to say that evil grew only when the ground had been prepared by those small wars. Where was that brother who argued so passionately for peace, now? Was he caught up in some small war such as he'd talked about? Until today, none of us would have believed what had happened to him possible. We were afraid. With each mile we travelled I felt we were coming closer to an unnameable dread thing. And I did not want to be part of any of it.

Glancing sideways at Calypso, I saw with painful comprehension how thin the demarcation line between cruelty and decency was. How little time there always was to prepare; to pack up our lives, to flee from trouble before it arrived. The car sped silently onwards. Along the dual carriageway, past a deep forest of trees laced with snow, which hung on fences and in the locked-up park. There were lorries and trailers abandoned in the lay-bys like dead blackbirds. Nature's chilling indifference to human affairs was in evidence everywhere. Home as we knew it had vanished. Hektor was threading his beads and, yes, I felt sorry for him, too. Of all of us he was coping the worst.

7.

One afternoon during those first weeks, the cat began complaining loudly. Do you remember, Raphael? I was drawing you, concentrating hard but you were frowning, looking annoyed, spoiling my drawing.

'I'm sick of him,' you muttered and then you stood up.

I threw my pencil down.

'It's just a bloody cat,' I said. 'Why have one if you don't like cats?'

'I didn't want one,' you snapped. 'The Cretino chose me.'

You glared at me and I grinned because I knew exactly what you were thinking! You found me as much of a nuisance as the cat, didn't you?

'I tolerate the animal,' you announced.

'Really?'

That stopped you in your tracks and you stared suspiciously at me over the top of your glasses. I burst out laughing. Instantly you were on guard and, although the muscles of your face relaxed, you refused to smile.

'Yes, really.'

For several days after that I watched you when you fed the cat. If you thought I was watching there was a false roughness to your gestures that didn't convince either the cat or me. If you thought I couldn't see, you would stroke it. The cat gave the game away by purring loudly.

We carried on in this way for a few more days.

'I prefer cats to dogs,' you said, eventually and with some serious consideration.

You paused, glancing at me, trying to gauge my reaction.

'I hate dog-like devotion,' you added, raising your voice.

'Hmm,' I said.

Referring to me, are you? I thought, refusing to catch your eye. But then, just before we resumed our session, you hesitated, and you smiled as if I had caught you out. Somehow that smile – which was the first one directed at me – was so intimate that I blushed. Crazy. Neither of us spoke for the rest of that session.

My first painting took six weeks to get to some sort of decent state. I worked all the time and soon started another one. The sunshine and the warmth of the previous weeks had gone as swiftly as it had come and the rain and low clouds descended once more. One day I asked you if you'd let me draw you by candlelight. I told you I wanted to put some shadows on your face and could only do this at night. Really it was an excuse to see you in the evening.

'You don't need to add any shadows,' you said, sounding annoyed again. 'I already have plenty on my face. At my age it is impossible to live without shadows.'

I was a bit staggered by the remark but said nothing and a day or two later, reluctantly, you agreed to let me visit in the evening.

'I suppose you want something to drink,' you said when I arrived, by way of greeting.

'Tea would be nice. Shall I make it?'

You looked affronted. You weren't senile. You could make tea. But then you took out something stronger from the cupboard.

'Are you allowed to drink wine?'

'I do what I like,' I said sharply and it was your turn to grin.

Ah! Your look said. Goal!

Your house was so different at night. It had a different geography attached to it, which I could not place but recognised. Calypso, too, was able to recreate some *otherness* with little effort in a similar way. When I tried to say this to you, Raphael, you merely grunted and poured us both another glass of wine. I didn't draw much that first night. The wine had gone to my head. I giggled.

'What's the joke?'

I shook my head.

'My father would have a fit if he could see me now,' I said.

'Perhaps you should go?'

'Oh God! Don't you start.'

'Of late, have you noticed there are no stars?' you said, changing the subject.

It made you restless, you admitted, without saying why. What was this obsession of yours?

'The nights are too long,' you complained, fretfully.

Well then, I wanted to say, let me stay with you.

Of course I didn't say any such thing or you might have exploded.

'Why don't you read?' I asked instead.

'Because books are expensive and hard to come by.'

This was true. No one had noticed it happening, but bookshops had slowly become things of the past. Only the elderly who had lived in one place all their lives had books.

'I moved too often,' you volunteered and I pricked up my ears at this small snippet of information. 'I don't have many books. Besides, my sight is bad.'

'Stop acting as if you are an old man.'

There was a pause as you considered what I had just said. Then you brought out a dish of salt cod. You put two colourful plates on the table and some cutlery. You rummaged in the cupboard for bread. Your one friend was a Jewish baker in the old part of the nieghbourhood. The bread there was always wonderful but once, when I took some home, Hektor went crazy.

'What's the matter with you? Don't you know these Jews hate us,' he shouted. 'Don't ever bring that filth into this house again.'

That was my father. Every inch of him a bigot!

'Have some bread,' you said, breaking into my thoughts.

You reached over for my plate and I stared again at the long scar across your arm. I was curious but didn't dare ask how you'd got it. There was so much about you that was mysterious in those early days and it was this that made you so fascinating.

Over the next few weeks we got into a pattern. I sketched you in the day during the hours you'd allow me and, in the evening, I transferred the sketches onto canvas. One of my tutors was going crazy about this work.

'Hera, you are blossoming!' he said, excitedly.

But, Raphael, you showed not the slightest interest in what I was doing. You remained mulish and bad-tempered. To tell you the truth, I was beginning to get fed up. Our sessions were conducted mostly in silence with you gazing towards the window. There were two photographs pinned to the wall, of a man and a woman, but if I so much as glanced at them your irritation rose like a cloud.

Then out of the blue, six months after I had first met you and just before your flu, you started talking to me. Do you remember?

'I am a product with a manufacturing defect,' you said.

I was taken aback. Was this some sort of joke?

'I am surrounded by people who have no manufacturing defects, which makes mine more obvious.'

When I said nothing you added, 'Will you put this into your painting?'

'I am not that good a painter,' I said at last in a small voice. 'To see into someone's soul isn't easy.'

And I remember I had laughed nervously. Then, because the conversation was going in that direction, I told you the painting was turning out to be mostly in shades of white. This seemed to please you. And after that you began to really relax. And that was when I thought, yes, my instincts are right. This *will* be a good painting.

A strange thing happened a few days after this conversation. I was late and, instead of your usual irritation, you had a distinct air of anxiety that I noticed when I arrived. You had been sitting at the kitchen table with a piece of paper and a pen in front of you but you didn't seem to have written anything on it. Instead when I pushed open the door you looked up and said '*Hera!*' as though I had been away for days. It had begun to thunder. I was soaking wet. You stared at me and then (unusually) helped me off with my coat. Next you gave me an orange towel with which to dry my hair. After that you made me a glass of sage tea. I was taken aback by all the attention. Our hands brushed briefly as you handed me the glass and I saw you looking at my hair.

In the silence that followed you raised your hand and touched it. In the culture I had grown up in the touching of a woman's head is an anointment.

And it was in this silence, too, that, reluctantly, I admitted to myself that I had fallen in love.

It turned out to be a good session. I painted two small watercolour sketches of your head. The curly greying hair was easy to do but your eyes were harder. For something to say, I foolishly started questioning you.

'Why d'you have a collection of shake-and-snow domes?' I asked, my voice not quite its usual self.

They were from different cities: Paris, Rome, Antwerp, Venice.

'Have you been to *all* these places?'

'No,' you said abruptly and the subject was dropped.

Right at the end of the session when it was nearing eleven o'clock you spoke.

'I died long ago,' you said. 'I'm just waiting for my turn to be buried.'

I was so shocked that my hand started to shake and I couldn't work any more. I made some excuse, saying I was tired. You nodded. You, too, were tired, you said, but still you insisted on walking me back to my small room. This was a first. I cried myself to sleep that night without knowing why.

The next day I was reluctant to visit you. I had not been to college for days. What was the point of these drawings? What was the point of trying to make friends with a man like you? What on earth was the matter with me? A kind of depression descended on me. The weather too was closing in. And at about four o'clock I suddenly made up my mind and went over to see you, knowing you would be waiting. I was determined to start a fight. And what did *you* do? Before I could begin my fight you gave me a piece of amber. It was round and smooth and deeply coloured. Shocked, I felt my heart rise. Without quite looking at me you said it came from a village in the desert; a village that was fading away from your mind. Were you having some private joke at my expense, Raphael?

'There are all manner of things in the wasted heart of that country,' I remember you said.

'In the desert?' I asked.

'The desert isn't empty, there are minerals and precious stones if you look for them.'

I noticed your voice had become unsteady.

You took my hand and put the amber in the palm of it. When you closed my fingers around it I had the strangest feeling you were telling me something of great significance.

'This is for you,' you said.

Something hard shifted on the shelf of my heart. Later that night, when I was alone in my studio, I took the amber out of my pocket and looked at it. And then I started crying again because I remembered the other thing you'd said.

'You must not expect too much of me.'

And when I looked at you in disbelief at what I'd heard you shook your head.

'I mean it,' you said.

8.

The light went. The snow-sky closed in on us. Opening the front door, we stared. Hatred glinted back at us from every corner of our home. We had fled to the police station, forgetting all else, and only now did we see the extent of the damage. It had been a night of broken glass. Someone had smashed the window in the downstairs cloakroom. Had this happened before or after we'd left? The anger was breathtaking. Without taking his coat off, Lyle began sifting through the glass while Hektor went in search of plywood to board the window up. The two of them ignored each other but Lyle showed no sign of wanting to leave and for this I was thankful. I didn't want to be alone with either of my parents.

'I'm cold,' Calypso murmured.

'Turn the heating up, then.'

Lyle continued sweeping up the glass.

'It's shock,' he said. 'You haven't eaten. You need to eat.'

Calypso just stood in the middle of the room and, in the end, I was the one who turned up the heating. The rest of them were in a trance. Hektor was banging away at the plywood much harder than he needed to. No one said anything.

'Sit down,' I told Calypso. 'I'll make us something to eat.'

I went into the kitchen and filled the kettle. Then I put

some couscous to steam. As I was shredding the cabbage, Lyle came in hurriedly.

'Are you staying?'

I nodded. What else did he think I would do? Even if I had wanted I couldn't leave. By now the snow had been falling in thick suffocating waves for a few hours but it felt more like days. There was something intense and malevolent about the speed in which the roads were being covered. There was no way I could get back on foot to my room. The buses weren't running at this hour and, in any case, I could not leave with everything still so unresolved. Lyle looked relieved. A cat ran across the back garden and the light outside was activated. I saw small paw prints going across the white ground. The hammering in the sitting room stopped and Hektor walked through the kitchen and out to the garden shed.

'I'm going to have to replace the lock on the front door when the shops open,' he said loudly without looking at us.

The garden light came on again. More footprints across the snow. The door of the shed opened and shut and there was a sharp blast of freezing air as Hektor returned, stamping snow from his feet. He hesitated, glaring at me. Then he sighed and seemed about to speak, changed his mind and shook his head sourly. I began to fry the cabbage. I added cumin and parsley and tomato puree and salt. And a few chopped onions. I could not find the garlic. I looked in the fridge and found some pieces of mutton so I added these to the mix.

Lyle waited until Hektor was out of earshot.

'Listen, Hera,' he whispered. 'You're going to have to look after her if she is to get through the night.'

I was silent. The stew bubbled. Suddenly there just wasn't enough air in the room. I felt my energy draining away. I knew what was coming. It was what I had been dreading. Hektor and Calypso, both back in my life again in spite of everything I had done to shake them off. I stared at my hands. My parents and I had not seen eye to eye for years. I had falsely believed that all their stupid struggles, their unhappiness, had ceased to be my concern. They were no longer *my* problem I had thought. But here they were, back again, ready to steal my freedom. Just when I thought I had escaped. My eyes filled up. I didn't want to think of Aslam. Whatever it was that he had done, whatever he was up to, the senseless stupid risks he might have taken, these things were *not* my problem. Yes, Aslam, I thought, bitterly, this is so typical of you. No consideration for anyone except yourself. Lyle was looking hard at me. He knew exactly what was going on in my head but for Lyle there was nothing more important than Calypso. He would do anything for her and that included sacrificing me if need be. Well, how great was that! I put the lid on the pan and went outside without answering him. I wondered if my asthma was starting up again.

When I got back into the kitchen, I could hear them arguing in the lounge. Someone had switched on the small light and drawn the curtains. I knew Hektor had begun cursing Aslam and I felt guilty because hadn't I been doing just that a moment ago? I felt small-minded and ashamed. We none of us knew the truth of it. How could we blame him?

'Ah!' Hektor said, seeing me. 'Praying at last, are you?'

He brushed past me and took two glasses from the cupboard. Oh good, I thought, going to start drinking, are we? That's going to help a lot. Calypso came in next and poured herself a glass of water. I heard her swallow and, going over to her, I put my arm around her. None of this was her fault.

'Where's Lyle?'

'On the phone.'

And Hektor would soon be drunk. There was nothing much else to say. I stared out of the window, feeling sick and paralysed, only dimly aware that Calypso was speaking. I wanted desperately to go to you, Raphael, sit in your kitchen, tease you and watch your reluctant smile. Calypso raised her voice.

'What?'

'Yesterday morning,' she said, 'before they took Aslam. I'm telling you, a very strange thing happened. You know, I was standing just here as we are, as I do every morning, scanning the sky for the bird. You know who I mean?'

I nodded, forcing myself back into the present. For the past few months Calypso had been feeding a large bird. It was a bird of prey, an eagle owl I think they call them. Calypso loved all birds and in particular those birds of prey that overwintered in the Middle East. So when this one arrived out of nowhere to rest on the bird table, she started feeding it bits of leftover meat.

'Whenever he came I felt – well – exhilarated. You know?'

I made a noncommittal sound.

'As if some person had given me a gift.'

I sighed. My chest felt as taut as a violin string. I'd heard all this many times before and it bored me but I nodded. At least she was talking.

'He used to drop small presents outside the kitchen door before he would eat the chicken I put out for him.'

I pulled a face. I hadn't liked the bird. The things it brought were actually body parts: hideous torn pieces of an animal's leg; a wing; a cross-section of a neck with the blood still fresh; prey that he had caught. Yet I also knew that, in spite of the macabre nature of the offerings, Calypso wasn't at all squeamish. Aslam had known about this ritual too but he'd found it funny whereas I found the whole business disgusting.

'You know, I always had the feeling the bird and I were involved in a conversation of some sort.'

Conversation!

'You know, five small pieces of fresh chicken for a body part. A fair exchange, huh? I had a strange feeling that bird came from the marshes near my grandparents' home.'

Ah! I thought. She's never said that before but, obviously, this is what it's all about.

'Then yesterday morning,' Calypso said, raising her voice a little, 'I saw the bird again. I had not seen him for almost a week. In fact, I had begun to wonder if he'd migrated because of the snow. But suddenly there he was again, swooping down from his usual direction. Only, instead of landing on the feeder, he came crashing against the kitchen window.'

I raised an eyebrow.

'His wings made a shadow over the sky for a second and he thudded against the glass. It sounded like a gunshot. He gave a terrible scream and then he vanished.'

I wondered if she was making this up.

'I know you don't believe me but Hektor heard it too.'

'So? Had it been shot?'

Calypso shook her head.

'Hektor opened the back door and found it. It was lying on its side. Your father picked it up with the shovel and put it in the wheelie bin.'

I didn't know what to say but I knew what was coming.

'We were both upset. You know why?'

'Yes. But you must know it's all nonsense. You live here now, Mum. All that stuff … it's …' I hesitated, 'it's *medieval*.'

'You don't know what you are saying,' Calypso shouted. 'You see what's happened, you see? It's a bad omen.'

I groaned. Didn't we have enough to worry about without these old superstitions?

'Hektor has been washing his hands all day,' Calypso said, lowering her voice, ignoring me.

You bet, I thought. With Hektor, cleanliness always reaches a new height at times of fear.

'He didn't work today,' Calypso said. 'I think he spent most of the time praying. And now this has happened.'

In spite of my good intentions, and my desire to break free from her stupid superstitions, I, too, shivered.

'People here don't understand,' she said, fiercely. 'Wild birds should be left alone; no one should hurt them.'

I was silent.

'When a bird of prey dies it's a curse,' she went on.

And then, when I remained silent, she began to sing.

9.

Aslam and I had always known about our mother's great love. The story had been the backdrop to our childhood. I have no idea who told us. Maybe we overheard the adults gossiping when we were small; maybe Calypso, after one of her fights with Hektor, told Aslam and he told me. Perhaps it was our mother's way of punishing Hektor for being so stupid or perhaps it was simply her way of making sure the story lived on within us. I was neither shocked nor interested. It was just something I'd always known. But I now believe that, deep down, both Aslam and I had been profoundly influenced by the story. How else could I account for Aslam's crazy idealism or the way I felt about you, Raphael? Growing up with Calypso's romance had made romantics of us both.

Our mother had been in love with Lyle and he with her. It had happened long before she met Hektor of course. At the time Calypso had been visiting her grandparents in a small, beautiful village not far from her beloved marshes. The village used to be called the Venice of the desert. The story began one day when Lyle, then only a boy, saw her by chance on a crowded street. Calypso had been out with a relative. It was the time of the almond blossom. There were pink petals drifting everywhere over the waterways, framing the faces of the young girls, making them look more lovely than usual.

Calypso was beautiful anyway but that spring when Lyle first saw her she must have been stunning. She was a tall girl with enormous dark eyes. Because she was veiled he did not see her hair but from the way it moved inside her hijab he suspected it would be long and glossy and he fantasised about it endlessly.

Every day after that initial glimpse Lyle went back to the same spot to wait, hoping to catch sight of her. He became obsessed with her and if a day passed when she did not appear he was in despair, unable to eat or sleep – or so the story goes. Given my own obsession I am inclined to believe this! One day he managed to pass her a note. How mundane, how unoriginal? Yes. But you must understand that in such a place, at such a time, only the brave could dare do a thing like this. A girl could be stoned to death and a boy whipped for lesser offences. Calypso read the note and what followed was also predictable. Lyle was handsome but poor and in that place, and in those days, money counted. Poor Lyle didn't have a chance.

Their affair was slow and difficult and was conducted only in the months when Calypso visited her grandparents. Here she had a little more freedom but she was a very superstitious girl and there were always sinister omens surrounding her meetings with Lyle. On one occasion he stepped on a poisonous spider that bit his big toe. On another, a large bird of prey flew down from a date palm and perched on a nearby wall where it stared at them balefully. Calypso firmly believed the birds were bringers of bad luck. Lyle used to tease her about this, then and now. Thank God there is at least one person I know who isn't living in the Stone Age.

One day, when the two of them were hiding amongst the reeds, talking, one of these birds dropped a half-eaten water vole at Lyle's feet. After that, Calypso insisted they avoid that stretch of water and go elsewhere to a more remote island. Lyle agreed of course. He would do anything to make her happy. But the bird still flew over towards them as though it was hunting them out. The idea petrified Calypso and, although they were wild for each other, the hopelessness of their situation was beginning to dawn on her. The intensity of their attraction was wearing Calypso down. The marshes *were* beautiful but summer was passing swiftly. Soon Lyle, who was six years older, would have to go to the big city to take the exams needed to win a university scholarship. It was, he told Calypso, his only hope of having a different sort of life from that of his fisherman father. In the city the idea of a young man and a girl being alone in this way would have been unheard of. But partly because of her grandparents' unusually progressive ways, Calypso was allowed to do as she pleased. The day would be their last together.

They had gone out in the *mashuf* belonging to Lyle's uncle very early in the morning. Lyle paddled the canoe with the butt end of the fish spear dipping in and out of the water. The sun was slowly rising through the mists as they glided through the shallows. The sky was a pale, luminous blue, touched here and there with semi-transparent wisps of clouds. Bulrushes grew all around. A few buff-backed herons, grave as imams, hunched and brooding, sat watching the river traffic, while small coots and cormorants swam noisily about. There was no sign of the bird of prey. The reed beds were very high at that time of year with giant grasses growing to almost twenty-five feet, pale gold and silvery grey except at the base where they were very green. Lyle steered the *mashuf* out of the reeds and on towards a small sheltered lagoon.

He knew those waterways like the back of his hand and knew of a place where they would not be disturbed. So they moored the canoe and stepped onto the *tuhul*. A *tuhul* is a small floating island with sedge and brambles and mint and willow herb. A *tuhul* is a magical place and after she left the marshes Calypso would never see one again. All day, through the long summer afternoon, they stayed on their *tuhul*. They stayed talking and cuddling each other, returning home only as the sun began to set. And as their old boat glided silently through the dusk-lit waters of the marshes, they heard a boy's lilting voice singing an old Arab love song. For Calypso it was an omen. Their lives would never be the same again.

According to my mother a girl's future was predictable. Marriage, arranged to someone unknown, followed by children, was all there was to look forward to. The fortune-teller told her family she was only interested in the palms of Calypso's brothers. Suddenly all her hopes, the books she read, the idea that one day she would become a doctor, the arguments of right versus wrong that she had with her family were as nothing.

And that was that. My poor mother was whisked away and a marriage was duly arranged between her and the man they called Hektor. The man destined to become my father. She left for London with her new mini-cab-driving husband and very soon encountered a whole different set of problems. Hektor worked long hours, leaving early and returning home late. Calypso, who was beginning to feel the cold bite of loneliness, was soon pregnant. With nothing to do, she began to sink into a slow depression.

Time altered things. The old maps, the borders of the past began to vanish even before the politicians messed everything up. Even before the snow came. What was left was a fine cross-section through time. Fifteenth and twenty-first centuries intermingled uneasily in the white city.

'I know of no woman who comes from my country who is happy here,' Calypso told me once.

Seven years would pass before she and Lyle would meet up again. Long enough for the entire planet to change. And it was chance that brought them together. A chance taxi ride. Lyle, sitting in the back of Hektor's car, recognised something familiar about him. Lyle spoke to Hektor in dialect and Hektor answered, unsurprised. Nothing about his passengers surprised him after fourteen years of driving taxis. He didn't even bother to look in his mirror, not until Lyle asked him if he was the boy who had married Calypso. Boy! By then Hektor was no boy. Still, he took Lyle home to meet her, which was something. Cunning Hektor, always looking out for the main chance. Lyle was educated, had a good job, money, too, and Hektor saw immediately that he would be a useful person to know.

I remember coming home from school and seeing Calypso crying. It made me sad at the time but I remember that Aslam just got angry and stormed out. Lyle was an archaeologist by now. He was a man of endless curiosity and clear sensibilities, not a bit like Hektor. Before long Aslam and I fell under his spell and grew to love him. A couple of years ago, when there was the trouble over the business of my going to art school, it was Lyle who supported me, argued with Hektor and came with me to see the school. That was the kind of forward-thinking man he was. Not like my bloody father, I mean. When I told Lyle that I wanted to be a painter he asked me, 'What sort of things will you paint?' He didn't sneer at the idea as Hektor had done. And now look how he's helping us. Lyle. Where would we be without him?

10.

Ten at night. The snow had not let up. Hektor turned the television on but the talk was simply about the weather and nothing else. Unconsciously, I suppose, we had expected it to be about *our* news. Nobody had eaten the mutton stew; nobody was hungry and tomorrow or the next day the congealed remains would end up in the bin. I was just wondering whether I should do the washing up, make more tea, perhaps, when there was a knock on the door. There stood a few of Hektor's cronies covered in snow. They came in cautiously, glancing nervously at Calypso, knowing she hated them, but she just stalked off into the kitchen on this occasion without saying a word. Hektor avoided her eye. He brought out a pipe and it was passed round. Arak was poured. The high priest of all knowledge was holding forth and ignoring the women. The press, he told the room, had been outside all evening, like a pack of dogs at the ready.

'Tomorrow's news,' he shouted, 'that is when the trouble will start. You wait and see. Tomorrow that bastard will make a statement.'

He was referring to the Prime Minister.

'We are at the beginning of a global crisis,' one of the men said in English. 'This thing with your boy is just the beginning. Watch out! Everything will get worse.'

Helpful of him, I thought, angrily. Trust Hektor to ask these old fools to visit at a time like this.

'This is God's way of punishing the unbeliever! Remember the floods. *Seven* months, all over the country. The human race is finished.'

I watched from the doorway. Why did he need to shout so much? Couldn't someone tell him to shut his stupid mouth? The fact was, as a community, we were caked in hopelessness, a people under attack. And how we loved to make things worse for ourselves. Lyle must have been thinking something along the same lines because he stood up, refusing the pipe, and followed Calypso into the kitchen. I felt a hand on my shoulder. It was Iris. She had the soft look of a woman with no power whatsoever. I remembered how Aslam and I used to joke about her. We called her the Bird Interpreter because of her superstition around the subject of birds.

'I came back as soon as I could,' she said. 'Where is she?'

'Calypso? In the kitchen with Lyle.'

Iris had a son Aslam's age. She nodded, meaning I didn't have to elaborate. She knew all about my mother's past life. I think that in a way Iris envied it, knowing she would never have had the courage to live as her friend had done.

'You know, Scylla came to see me this afternoon.'

Scylla was an old woman who lived a few streets away. She read the coffee grains. Oh yes, we were still surrounded by the fears of many centuries. There was little hope of ever scraping it off our shoes.

'She heard what happened,' Iris whispered. 'She didn't want to come over this evening and bother you. And she saw the journalists outside … but she does want to speak to Calypso.'

I felt annoyed. It was clear that apart from Lyle and me everyone was looking for more ways to upset Calypso. Was this some sort of endurance test or something?

'You never know. She might be able to help you all …'

'Look,' I said, and I took a deep breath. 'Calypso is very upset. She … we don't want any speculation at this point, you know?'

Iris looked hard at me. 'You okay?' she asked, suddenly.

I made a small surprised sound. No one had asked *me* how *I* felt. Everyone except poor simple Iris had assumed I was fine. So I smiled at her. There wasn't much wrong with Iris, I thought. She was a kind woman who had been repressed by a husband who beat her and had mutilated her daughter. Was it surprising that Iris was timid?

'I think you should talk to Calypso,' I said, finally. 'But be careful.'

The kitchen was in a mess. Lyle stood by the back door talking to Calypso. When he saw us, he frowned. Whatever they were saying was not for our ears. I had a definite sense of unease and the growing certainty that at least one of them knew something about Aslam they were not prepared to come out with. Iris went over to Calypso and gave her a hug. She did not, of course, touch Lyle.

'I came as soon as I could,' she said.

Lyle nodded.

'I'll leave you two to talk, then,' he said. 'I have to make a few phone calls.' He looked anxiously at Calypso. 'Will you be okay?'

Calypso didn't answer.

'I'll be back by first light and if I hear any news I'll ring, okay?'

She nodded vaguely.

'Try to get some sleep, even if only for a couple of hours. You'll see him tomorrow, I promise.'

'You made cabbage soup?' Iris asked as soon as he had gone. 'Hera, was it you? Have you gone mad?'

'It was a mutton stew, that's all.'

Here we go, I thought wearily, more fucking superstition.

'Throw it away,' Iris cried in dismay. 'No one has died!'

'Oh piss off,' I said under my breath.

I wanted to punch her, to shout, to run out of the house. I felt as though I was drowning in my childhood. My whole life has been one long struggle to survive, I wanted to scream at them both. Being born in the West isn't enough. You fools, can't you see what you have done to a whole generation? You have taken away our freedom, I wanted to say. Don't for one moment think that your birthplace gives you automatic freedom. And then I thought, I have a mother who has never mixed with anyone who isn't an Arab. What freedom is there in that? Birth and freedom are two separate things, you idiots, I wanted to yell. I have a British passport, British nationality, British accent. And what does that amount to? Can you blame Aslam if he *has* taken a different path to freedom?

Of course I didn't say anything.

'You need a *good* lawyer,' Iris was saying. 'Not that white man Lyle has hired. You need someone who isn't one of *them*.'

Ah, so it's them and us again, I thought, working myself up into a silent fury. So what about this multicultural cohesive society we were supposed to have? The one the Prime Minister was always banging on about?

'Shall we go and see Scylla tomorrow?' Iris asked.

But Calypso was miles away. Ignoring Iris, she turned to me.

'I am tired,' she said. 'How many things do I have to do battle with? The establishment, my husband, the imam, the police, the press, thoughts of my son's deceit?'

I took a deep breath. I was trembling with the effort of keeping silent. My heart was pounding.

'Stop it!' I said quietly.

'I want to run away,' Calypso murmured. 'I want to return to where I belong.'

She seemed in a trance. 'It's the marshes I want. I want to wade out into the reeds and listen to the wind rattling. The wind made the reeds sound like teeth in a skull. I want to listen to the water birds calling to each other at dusk and hear the oars of the *mashuf* dipping into water. And I want to creep back to my grandmother and hear her loud laugh.'

We were silenced.

Outside, through the window, we heard Lyle trying to start his car over and over again.

I swallowed nervously. A few nights ago Aslam had phoned me. I had told no one about this but Aslam had not been himself. For some reason he started raging about those unknown relatives of ours killed in the marshes during the civil war. We all knew that Calypso's grandparents had been hacked to death. Arabs killing Arabs was old news so my brother's anger had at first puzzled me.

'I am the self-appointed bearer of a history no one wants to hear,' he'd said.

'What?' I'd asked, annoyed. 'What's the matter with you?' I had been about to visit you, Raphael, and now I would be late.

'You, dear sis, have been brainwashed by the British,' he declared.

He sounded drunk and not for the first time I wondered if he'd been taking drugs. I hadn't known what he meant but the violence of his anger had scared me. Was he *blaming* the British for the civil war in that region? Had he some grand plan to punish the people of this country, and us too in the process? If so, I now thought, no coffee-cup reading would help us. His sins would be our sins. I badly needed to speak to him.

Calypso began humming to herself. Iris stared at her. She did not come from the same tribe as Calypso. She had no understanding of the way marsh people felt about their home.

'When my grandfather was killed,' Calypso said loudly, 'my mother sat beside his body all day until dusk fell. I remember the smoke from the buffalo-dung bonfire hanging like a veil across her face. Maybe I should not have spoken of these things to my own children. Maybe it is my fault. I am afraid that I have given them the burden of the past.'

I closed my eyes. Oh God, I thought. She *does* know something. Aslam *has* told her what he's up to. So what is she hiding?

The voices of the men in the next room rose and fell. The television droned on and outside the snow continued falling softly. Without warning, Calypso began to cry.

'That bird,' she said, 'it left its prey for me before it died.'

11.

Love came to us as a winter story, Raphael. I think we both knew this. And daily, as the snow increased, we drew closer. As you know, drawing involves the intimacy of the eye and hand as it travels across a face. Add to that the fine lead of a pencil and you have touch. From this it could be said that I fell in love with a pencil in my hand. But, even as the icy wind began bringing down snow blossoms from the trees, you tried to keep yourself aloof. What demons were you fighting? I knew you were frightened, but of what was ambiguous. Our hands barely touched and when they did it was more often than not by accident. Yet accidental contact was extraordinarily sweet and I longed for more of it. I had begun to play little tricks on you. Did you know?

'Feel how cold my hands are,' I said on one occasion.

Or, 'Look how blue my fingers got.'

Or, 'My ears are *so* cold!'

And then in desperation, 'Are you cold?'

But each time the response was unsatisfactory. Raphael, you were too clever for me. Each time you simply offered me some gloves, put another log on the fire, suggested I cover my head (cover my head, after all the trouble I took to keep my head uncovered). But you would not touch me.

I decided to try something new. I decided to talk to you while I drew. No questions, I decided. Since you show no curiosity I'll tell *you* things about myself, you rat. That was the plan.

'My parents' neighbourhood is a place of lost hopes and failure. Any optimism that once existed fled years ago,' I said.

I spoke casually.

'Perhaps the reason I hate going back is because I can't ever remember a time when the place was happy. Life on our street has always been a row of dreary satellite-television dishes and shrunken lace curtains with waterless vases of plastic flowers.'

You blinked, a look of astonishment on your face.

'Even the snow which should be sugar-white and beautiful when it falls in our garden looks dirty.'

I was joking but you had a serious look on your face.

'Don't say things like that,' you reprimanded me. 'Your parents are from a different sort of place. It will have been hard for them to live a happy life.'

I digested this in silence. Were you talking from personal experience?

'My mother says it wasn't always like this,' I said, ignoring your tone of voice.

I was annoyed. Somehow you always managed to make me feel like a stupid child. So I told you, in a slightly superior way, how it used to be in the white city. You, after all, hadn't grown up here like me.

The city had already been christened 'white' by the Mayor because it was so clean. Snow was still a long way away.

'No sun, of course, but no weird weather either. Then, when I was about four or five, the rubbish burning started. First the councils started burning the mountains of plastic that had accumulated and next it was the rotting animal carcasses. Soon there were sludge fields all across the country. No one in the cities took much notice. But then the stories of the animal diseases started spreading and the butchers' shops began to smell of hoof glue. Calypso became alarmed. There was nothing for it but to stop eating meat, even from the animals slaughtered in the sacred way.'

You pulled a face but you were still listening, interested. The stench, I told you, was unbearable.

'The news was about nothing else. Children were dying awful deaths. Their last breath came out as a terrible bovine moan. We were all petrified. What if we had the disease, too?'

For an industrialised country it was shameful that no one had detected this plague sooner. The various councils hadn't bothered until it was too late. Their greedy indifference had made them cut corners. And they claimed that the money spent on every small war had left them with no reserves.

'Aslam and I were children,' I said. 'That was when the new viruses started arriving at our school. Two children died in my class because, the headmaster told us in assembly, these viruses were drug-resistant and dangerous.'

You looked up sharply.

'What d'you mean,' you asked in a low voice, staring at me. 'What did the authorities do? And how many children died?'

I had no idea. I had been just a child.

'Personal hygiene is important, was what we were told,' I said. 'Wash your hands.'

When Aslam came home and told this to Calypso she snorted with laughter.

'We Muslims are clean, you tell him,' she said. 'We even bury our dead as soon as possible!'

In the end, when the animal epidemic had reached its height, the authorities declared an emergency and began burning the dead animals instead of burying them. Huge bonfires sprang up in fields outside the busy towns and along the edges of motorways. 'This I remember very clearly,' I said. 'Hektor used to say that, on certain nights when he was driving a fare around, he could see the burning cattle, their poor stiff hooves piled in pyramids that reached up to the sky.'

I stopped talking. I had forgotten all that. There had existed an uneasy, precarious feeling that we kids picked up.

'When the smog started to appear, the activists said it was the plastics that were the problem. The plastics were bad for the environment. But others thought it was the burning flesh, killed before its time, that was a curse on the land.'

'Now, Raphael, the name White City seems apt in a different way.'

You nodded at the irony.

'Are you close to your brother?' you asked me.

'Yes. Why?'

You shook your head.

'No reason.'

'He went to Sheffield to study Psychology and Religion and, soon after, I escaped to art school.'

'Escaped?'

'Well, my father wanted a different path for me,' I said lightly.

How on earth could I tell you about Hektor? I hesitated. Then, just as I was about to ask if *you* had any brothers, you asked me if I'd like to stay to supper. At last, despite the dreadful weather my life was beginning, I thought joyously.

I can't remember now if that was the night you gave me the amber.

'Tell me about the desert,' I remember I asked, boldly, fortified by the wine I was drinking. 'You lived there once, didn't you?'

There was a long pause. I thought I had gone too far and I felt like crying.

'Yes,' you said, faintly, at last. 'I lived there once. It was hot and there were many stars. But let's not talk about that now. Tell me more about your family.'

12.

In the days that followed, our lives and the weather remained static. The press settled on us like a swarm of flies and refused to move on. Apart from the strangeness of this weather there was obviously nothing else of interest. The cold was no deterrent and they took to loitering on the other side of the street, skulking in the bushes, waiting for one or other of us to venture outside. I've no idea what narrative they hoped to piece together by watching us alone. Our faces revealed nothing and we merely ignored them.

My unhappiness was twofold. Naturally I was worried and upset about Aslam but I also desperately wanted to return to my own life. I had not seen you for days, Raphael, and it bothered me that you might be misunderstanding my silence. I had tried ringing you a couple of times but your phone seemed not to be working. Also, because of the surreal quality of our lives, I'd actually lost track of how many days had passed. We were a family in mourning, deeply shocked and disorientated. I imagined this was how the bereaved felt, only in our case bereavement was accompanied by a sneering world just outside our front door. Really, it was hard to describe how we felt and it dawned on me that it was possible to be alive and not exist at the same time.

The snow did not let up. It was a blizzard really, although the weathermen were too scared to use the word. In the day the snow's never-ending fall and the accompanying low aluminium sky made everything appear drab and hopeless. This savage beauty was beginning to terrify inhabitants of the city. There was no sun.

At the beginning of the second week of Aslam's absence, Calypso insisted on going out. She had been cooped up for days, waiting by the telephone, and could no longer stand it, so she went out to buy whatever stale vegetables she could find at the open market. Because of the shortage of food, everything was expensive now. But it was easier to buy expensive and probably infected meat than it was to get fresh vegetables. This was July for heaven's sake. The whole world was longing for the fresh spring greens of a year ago.

Where had the roses of my childhood gone, the fragrance of cut grass in our back garden? I longed for summer nights with the pale scented tobacco plants my mother used to say reminded her of the smells from her own childhood. I even longed to see Hektor sitting out on the step with his useless cronies smoking his pipe and arguing stubbornly about God. And the couscous that we would bring out mixed with mutton and apricots. Apricots.

Not all the riches of the world would give us apricots now.

Or peaches.

Or pears.

Or even the humble apple.

Although I wanted to, I didn't dare visit you, Raphael, in case Calypso saw me. So instead I decided to go to the outdoor market and help Calypso by carrying her shopping. This was what I was thinking as I walked out into the frozen street. The blizzard seemed to increase and the snow fell with a grim determination that I hated. A hoar frost was forming on the branches of the trees. My breath froze on the air. And although it was only three o'clock, the light was fading. I walked fast, avoiding the icy patches on the road, thinking about the painting I had been making of you, Raphael, and at first the shouting did not bother me. Then I saw a small group of boys, about fifteen years old, I suppose, throwing snowballs at each other. I imagined the schools must have closed early and they were having a bit of harmless fun.

I decided to walk around them so as not to get hit, but then I saw they were actually pelting a woman with snowballs. The woman was covered from head to toe in black, standing completely still, making no effort to run away, while the boys threw the hard round balls of snow, like grenades, towards her head and back. Laughing. And then, to my astonishment, I saw it was Calypso they were laughing at. I stood open-mouthed for a moment longer on that impassable street. Then, in a whirlwind of fury, I ran towards her, shouting such obscenities that the boys fled. But Calypso smiled at me for the first time since Aslam was taken and to my utter amazement began to sing.

'Stop it, for God's sake!' I cried. 'Have you finally gone completely bloody mad? What d'you think you are doing?'

Calypso just sang louder. Hysterically, I began to propel her away from the direction of the market (she had done no shopping of course) towards home. Then I saw she was wearing her bedroom slippers and this made me even madder.

'Calypso,' I screamed, 'what the fuck are you doing? Do you want to die? Is that what you want? To die rather than help Aslam?'

She continued to sing but, thankfully, the street had emptied. When we approached the back gate of our house, she stopped suddenly and turned to me with a stubborn, closed, sly look.

'Don't let those bastards see you beaten,' she said.

Her eyes were on fire. We glared at each other.

'When I sing all the misery goes from my heart,' she said.

I opened the gate and dragged her into the garden without a word. This was just too much, I wanted to cry.

The snow had covered everything: the broken washing machine, the bookshelf that Aslam had smashed during a long-forgotten row, the old ceiling fan – why on earth did they buy a ceiling fan? – and the heap of unused bricks from some aborted project. But the garden looked peaceful and uncluttered under it. The snow had levelled its mess and rendered the clutter into a state of calm loveliness. I was finding it difficult to breathe.

As soon as I shut the gate, Calypso began singing again.

'Shush!' I said. 'For God's sake, don't attract any more attention. What good is that going to do?'

'They stare at me as if I'm a wild animal let loose. So I laugh in their face.' Once inside the kitchen she began taking off her soaking clothes. 'I sing for them to understand I'm not afraid of them.'

I opened my mouth to speak then shut it again, defeated. What was the use?

'Go on, throw the snow at me. And I'll just sing even louder,' she said.

I could see she was getting into her stride and, knowing her temper, I said no more. Instead I decided to have a hot bath.

The police returned again that day and the next and we

were interviewed with scary, robotic monotony. Each time they arrived the press became excited. They stopped drinking their coffee in the nearby café and rushed out. There must have been an awful lot of undrunk coffee lying around. The police, going in and out of our house gathering more items of our clothing, the broken computers in the loft and even a pile of empty tins in the shed, ignored them. They were too busy with their endless questioning, writing everything we said in painfully slow handwriting. Lyle was out negotiating with the Home Office. And we still had no news of Aslam. As our confusion grew, the meaningless questions merely confused us further.

Where did Aslam get his pair of trainers?

How did he afford such expensive clothes?

Did I know where his jeans were made?

Had he travelled to the Middle East recently?

Why did he buy so many foreign-language newspapers?

I really cannot remember how many times we were asked the same questions. I felt certain they were trying to trick us. Perhaps I gave different answers each time without realising it. Perhaps what had happened was *my* fault. With no news the fight was draining out of us.

I had lost count of the number of nights Aslam had been absent. It felt like years. At some point later that day we heard a new word being bandied about in the press. The word was *radicalisation*. Radicalisation.

That word connected with long beards and white robes.

Prayers and beads.

And anger that springs out of nowhere.

Things we would never have associated with Aslam. If it hadn't been so frightening we would have laughed. Hektor put his head in his hands and Calypso started her wretched singing. The neighbours banged on the front door. The rollercoaster had started up once more.

'Shut the fuck up or we'll call the police.'

'No!' Calypso shouted.

She stood in the doorway and smiled.

'You go to hell and take your family with you,' she said.

And she sang louder. She was so angry that singing was just about the only thing she was capable of doing without causing serious bodily harm.

'You're drunk,' the neighbour said. 'It's a disgrace, living here in our country and breeding terrorists!'

Calypso looked at the woman. She filled the doorway. I knew her rage was monumental but when she spoke she was quietly suppressing it.

'I absolutely have the right to sing in my own house,' she said.

And she continued singing while shutting the door. I giggled.

That evening the Prime Minister made a statement. It was short and to the point and hinted at the enemies of the British people. Aslam wasn't mentioned by name but our location was. A few minutes after this carefully orchestrated speech with its veiled expression of the fear of beheading on our streets, a brick was thrown at our window. It narrowly missed Hektor, who sat watching the news. The glass fell everywhere.

'Don't react,' I shouted, but Hektor had already rushed to the front door.

Of course there was no one outside but there was a line of large footsteps leading up to the window.

'Call the police,' I said.

'No! Call Lyle!' Calypso said.

'Don't be stupid!' Hektor said.

'How the police behave depends on who they are dealing with,' Calypso said.

Hektor was shouting and so was I. If this could happen to us, what would be happening to Aslam? The little pocket of hope that had been sustaining us these last days was beginning to cave in. We went inside.

'Come away from the window!' Hektor cried.

Calypso began to sweep up the broken glass.

'A mother, even a bad one, always blames herself,' she said.

Her voice was deadly quiet now; her singing had stopped.

But it wasn't over yet. There were more sounds of breaking glass. First one and then another bedroom window shattered. The snow was inching its way into the house like a stealthy criminal. When the window in the small downstairs toilet broke, Hektor got through to the police but, although they told him someone would be with us soon, a car did not arrive until many hours into the night. We were finding out how easy it is to be on the wrong side of the law.

'And you *still* defend your bastard son after this,' Hektor said.

By way of answer Calypso began another song.

The night was blue and crystalline, and hard. Why were the police taking so long?

'What do you expect?' Calypso asked, pausing in her singing. 'You expect them to hurry?'

And her singing got louder again. Oh God! Aslam, I thought, do you know what havoc you've caused? My mobile phone went off in my bag and I began searching frantically. By the time I did locate it, it had stopped ringing of course and the number wasn't one I recognised.

Lyle arrived finally. He was shocked by the state of the house and the first thing he asked was where were the police.

'Police!' laughed Calypso. 'What police for people like us?'

Lyle took both her hands in his and spoke to her softly in Persian. He was only telling her to be patient but, in the midst of all the anger that surrounded us, the Persian sounded so pure.

'Come, why don't you rest a little?' he said. 'At least until the police come. Come, Hera. Come. Take her upstairs for a while.'

Because it was Lyle speaking to her, Calypso allowed me to take her upstairs without a murmur. On the bed was a quilt she had made many years ago with all the dresses she had worn as a child. I ran my hand over it, smoothing it out. Each piece was a memory that would die when Calypso died. I stroked the quilt. If we could speak of those memories, would we be hated less by others? But no one wants other people's memories any more than they want the shoes of the dead.

There was the sound of banging coming from downstairs. Hektor and Lyle were boarding up the windows for the second time. Tomorrow, once again, the house would be in darkness.

13.

The world was now entirely shrouded in snow. The dark pines that grew at the bottom of our garden stood bowed as though at a requiem. It was so cold that your breath was like a beard in the outdoor air. Time was standing painfully still and, in order to distract myself from thoughts of Aslam, I concentrated on past conversations I'd had with you, Raphael.

'I was born here, looking as if I had been born elsewhere,' I told you one night.

'You are still young,' you'd replied. 'The young don't need to belong.'

'That isn't true! What's the point of being a hotchpotch of cultural compromises?'

'The world is just a mirror in which people see bits of themselves,' you said.

'Stop patronising me,' I told you crossly.

You turned away but not before I saw the gleam in your eyes.

'So,' I shouted, 'you're laughing at me, are you?'

You shook your head.

'Nothing can be learnt from the events that happened before,' you said, enigmatically.

Oh God, you were a master at changing the subject, I

thought. And I didn't know *what* on earth you meant. I used to feel I would go mad trying to engage with you. Honestly, Raphael, what was I doing with a man who was so reluctant to let me into his life? I felt so many barriers between us. Many of the things we said to one another seemed to form in our mouths without much thought.

Do you remember the day I had forgotten to bring my sketchbook? I had been out shopping, looking for tomatoes, and after an endless search I found something that vaguely resembled them. They were scentless of course and would undoubtedly be tasteless too, for these days a lot of vegetables were grown in a chemical way. But I was so excited, so busy planning what I'd cook for you (if only I'd had some parsley) that I forgot my drawing materials. Anyway, when I arrived, I unpacked my pathetic purchases while you watched me with a strange expression on your face. Then we stood for a moment looking at the snow. The white city seemed to be eating itself, I thought.

'It's too dark to draw,' I said.

You nodded and, looking at you, I felt a pang. You looked so frail, so defeated. Even the tomatoes could not cheer you up. I moved closer, hoping you would touch me. But you had retreated restlessly into another world.

'Very soon I will be rehoused in a "social unit",' you said, quietly.

'What d'you mean?' I asked.

There is a cannibal in our midst, I thought, alarmed.

'Put in a box somewhere,' you said solemnly.

Were you teasing me?

'Don't talk like this!' I said.

'I don't want anything to eat,' you said.

This might be the end of love, I thought hopelessly. I was trying not to be dramatic but I felt depressed. I had spent about two hours hunting out the tomatoes and now you were telling me you weren't hungry.

'There is no place for me here,' you added, looking hard at me, your face unreadable.

Do you remember saying that? You lit your pipe and I gazed at your hands sadly. Your eyes were beautiful but perhaps it was hopeless. You were depressed and now I was becoming depressed too. I could not cure you. Whatever secret you guarded was clearly none of my business. Why depress myself? I thought. You simply were not interested in me. What was the point?

'I'd better go,' I said, finally.

You didn't seem to hear.

'The devil has settled between us,' you said, turning around sharply to look at me.

'What?' I had been trying not to cry and now I got angry. Which was better. 'What's that mean?'

'You aren't good for me,' you said, nastily – or so I felt.

'*Me?*'

I couldn't believe it.

'You're scared,' I mocked. 'A silly old man who's too scared to live. Be braver, live a little.'

I'd hit home.

'Enough,' you said, your face flushed.

I laughed.

'Get yourself a boyfriend. I saw you yesterday and the day before that. Don't you have homework?'

And when I screamed at you that homework was for children, you nodded. Triumphant.

'You see,' you said. 'I was right! Too young to be painting *me*, Lolita!'

The name sat between us. So that was the problem, was it? So you *are* falling in love after all, Raphael, I thought triumphantly. Don't try denying it. You are in no position to argue with me now.

14.

At midnight, after repeated phone calls that became more and more agitated, a police car drew up outside the house. It had stopped snowing and the air was crisp and still. The light of a million stars shone down on the city while on the radio a voice informed the world that a new galaxy had been found by the space shuttle *Gaia*. A frost was forming. Walking would be treacherous tomorrow. But the knock on the door that we had been waiting two hours for was not what we expected. Behind the two police officers was the man from next door.

'There she is,' he said. 'That's her. She's the one causing the disturbance, keeping my children awake.'

Even Hektor was astonished.

'What you saying?' Calypso demanded. 'Prove it I make disturbance? I sing, that's all.'

'Obscenities,' the man said. 'It's disgusting.'

'What's disgusting, you and your wife, having sex Sunday mornings? Late at night? Grunting? And I know you have another woman!'

I caught hold of her hand because I was afraid, but she shook me off impatiently. Calypso and Aslam were exactly the same. Neither could keep their mouths shut. When I was younger I used to think they both had a kind of death wish.

'We phoned you,' Hektor said, 'hours ago.'

For once he held his anger in check.

'And you come now? What about our windows?'

The policeman put his hand up in annoyance. You don't challenge these people unless you are mad, I thought.

'Look,' Lyle said reasonably.

But even Lyle was too angry to be trusted. There was a limit to his endurance too.

'We've been calling you for hours about the windows. It's absolutely freezing in here. The people who did this will have disappeared by now.'

At that there was another knock and this time the officers we had called arrived. There were now two cars parked outside, enough to give the whole neighbourhood a hell of a treat. Eventually, after a lot more shouting, the man from next door was persuaded to leave. His face suitably smug. Job well done, I imagined him telling his wife. Both sets of police looked sheepishly at each other. A policewoman took me aside. She wasn't unfriendly so I explained that Calypso only sang to hide her despair. Was that so wrong?

'Try to get her to sing softly, would you?' she said.

Didn't she see the irony of her words?

'Do you live with your parents?'

I shook my head, wanting to cry again.

'It's okay, love,' the woman said, relenting suddenly, 'this must be tough for you.'

She looked as if she might say more. In a different kind of world I suppose she might have.

They left soon after cautioning Calypso, and we were at last able to focus on the broken windows. Only the help had come too late.

Had we heard any sound before the first brick?

Had we seen anyone running away?

Did we think it was the same person who broke each window?

Did we think the boys who had pelted Calypso with snowballs could have been the culprits?

And finally:

Did we have any enemies?

Calypso began to laugh and the policeman turned to me. What was the joke? Calypso's shoulders shook. Didn't he know that the whole world hated us now?

'Aslam is nothing to do with us,' Hektor said, pompously. 'If it is true, what they are saying, then we want nothing to do with him, d'you understand? We are peaceful people.'

I was chilled by his words. How quickly we betrayed one another. At least the Christians had a name for people like Hektor. I glared at him. Judas, I thought. I felt sure that one day Calypso would leave him. I saw Lyle looking at me. *Did* he know something we didn't?

'The press are lying,' was all he said. 'The boy is innocent.'

Lyle was a man difficult to assess. I doubted he would betray those he loved.

After the second lot of police left, promising to 'look into the matter', Hektor started a row with Calypso. Whenever he felt threatened it was Calypso who bore the brunt of his fears.

'Christ!' I said. 'Don't fucking start.'

Hektor looked as though he might have a heart attack. His face was so comical that it made even Lyle smile. 'What did you say?'

'Oh, leave it out,' I said. 'Don't you have better things to make a fuss about?'

Hektor was afraid of me. I'd known this for years. My unpredictability scared him and he seldom argued with me any more. All that stopped after I left home. Poor, fragile dad. Left with nothing but his unanswered prayers.

'Aslam,' Calypso said, hopelessly.

Underneath her defiance she was falling apart.

'The fundamentalists in our society thrive on simple ideas,' Lyle said. 'You know, kill and you'll go to heaven; an uncovered head is disrespectful so you shall be killed. There is no complexity to the militant mind. So do you *really* believe Aslam has such a mind?'

I swallowed.

The two weird conversations we'd had sat heavily on my stomach, curdling and filling me with unease. For a normally sweet-natured boy, when he started sneering Aslam could be difficult to deal with. In that second conversation we'd been talking about the future, his and mine. I'd just said that, lately, he seemed without purpose and for some reason this had annoyed him.

'People should not have to plan for the future,' he'd said in a strange, arrogant way, not at all like his usual self. 'All we have is short-term memory.'

I thought he was being sarcastic. But in the light of what had happened I wondered now what he'd meant.

'You're talking rubbish,' I told him.

On that occasion, too, I'd known something wasn't quite right. But was this simply hindsight at work? The conversation had been late one afternoon. He'd wanted to come to my place and I'd made an excuse. He'd sounded so odd that I wondered if he'd been taking drugs. I'd been about to visit you, Raphael, and I hadn't wanted any probing questions when he was in this mood. But he had come round anyway and stayed long enough to smoke two cigarettes. When I asked for one, he looked shocked. My brother had his own set of double standards. He'd flicked through my drawings and turned around the two portraits that were facing the wall. He'd stared at them for a long time.

'Be careful,' I said sharply. 'They're still wet.'

I was annoyed at the way he felt he could do as he pleased with my stuff. Ignoring me, he slowly rolled a cigarette.

'And what about you, little sister? You with the beautiful hair that you do not hide.'

He was no longer angry. I had that effect on him. I suppose we loved each other in the way of siblings. Casually, without putting too much effort into it.

'Is this for posterity?' he asked.

And now he was laughing openly at me.

'Because if it is, let me remind you that nothing lasts.'

'That isn't what astronomers would say,' I told him.

'Yeah?'

I was silent.

'What astronomers do you talk to?' Aslam asked.

He continued to laugh. It had been the last conversation we had before he was taken from us.

It was almost one in the morning by the time the police left and, in order to shut out the misery in the house, I went outside. The thing I wanted was as unattainable as a distant star. There was no comfort from its light.

I stood in the garden for as long as I could bear to. If I had walked two streets away I would have seen the roof of your shed and the end of your telescope, Raphael. It was easy to be obsessed with the stars, I thought. They were too far away to demand any commitment of a person. A man could be safe with his stars, I thought, getting angry. There was no moon and the whole street was in a deep sleep when suddenly a light came on in the back bedroom and I saw Calypso and Lyle, their heads bent towards each other, standing by the one unbroken window. A moment later the light went out again and I heard footsteps. Lyle came outside. He looked absolutely haggard.

'I'm walking back,' he said. 'Calypso has gone to bed and Hektor is on a fare to the airport.'

He hesitated.

'Rather him than me,' I said, imagining what the motorway would be like with even more snow predicted.

Again Lyle hesitated.

'Try to get some sleep yourself,' he said at last. 'I know this is difficult for you in all sorts of ways …'

I nodded. Tomorrow was Friday.

'You'll be able to see him on Monday,' he said. 'I've had a phone call. The lawyer has finally got a promise. I'll get an exact time.'

This was a useless conversation. Why hope?

'Go in,' he said. 'Don't get cold. I have everything under control. We are making a request to the Home Office. So keep strong, for her sake please.'

I nodded.

At the gate, just as he left, Lyle turned and looked at me again.

'Hera, I *know* you are unhappy,' he said.

'What d'you mean?'

'Oh Hera, it's obvious. And anyway … I saw you.'

'Uncle Lyle,' I began.

'It's okay, Hera. We'll keep all these things to ourselves for now. There's too much other stuff, you know, going on.'

I nodded without saying a word. I had been trying all day to stop myself from crying. Lyle waved his hand rather helplessly in the air. And then he was swallowed up by the night.

15.

Calypso was shouting again. The singing had stopped but the shouting was worse. The neighbours were banging on the wall once more and I was frightened there would be another fight and then the police would be called.

'In the fifth millennium BC, Hera,' shouted my mother, 'a tribe of people moved down from the plateau and settled in the delta on the edge of the marshes. To understand me you must understand my ancestors, my history.'

She was standing by the back door, her face turned towards the neighbours. Anyone watching would see that she was deliberately needling them. Where the hell were Lyle and Hektor? I thought furiously. How was I supposed to handle this on my own? What was I supposed to do? I would have happily killed Aslam for doing this to us at that moment.

'Mum,' I cried.

She gave me a look.

'Where's my son?' she asked. 'I want him back.'

'I know,' I said softly.

I didn't know what to do. Perhaps I should ring the doctor's surgery, I thought. But then I remembered the free doctors worked only on Thursdays. This was a Friday. None of us had insurance so the private clinics were out of bounds.

'During all the centuries when the Middle East was prosperous,' Calypso said loudly, 'the people here were savages.'

This is great, I thought. This is just what we need at this point, a history lesson from my mum.

'We had a culture, you know; a life, fresh fish from the marshes, tall buildings made of reeds in the most intricate way.'

'Hmm,' I said noncommittally, avoiding her eye.

'Many tribes passed through that small beautiful piece of land: the Sumerians, the Assyrians, the Kassites and the Guti. The Persians came, as did the Greeks and the Romans and then, finally, the Arabs.'

I nodded, resignedly. Here we go again. Why is it, I wondered unhappily, migrants never, ever forget? It seemed to me they had memories that had enlarged to twice the size of any normal person's.

'That fertile earth had seen so much glory and chaos but it was our marshes that were the real refuge for the defeated and displaced people passing through them.'

Calypso, I thought, Lyle *will* get Aslam back. You know that. Will you allow yourself to finally let go of your stories? I am sick of them, sick of living in *your* past while my own present is disappearing. I wondered what she would say if I suddenly started talking about you, Raphael. Would she be interested, or was Aslam all there was in her world? I had grown up knowing my brother was more important than me. I wasn't jealous but, now and again, just occasionally, it would have been nice to be noticed by my family. In a positive way, I mean. You had said you were sure they noticed me, Raphael, but what did you know about the way we lived? You'd never met these crazy people.

'Are you listening, Hera?' Calypso asked.

'Yes,' I said. 'But you must come in now because we're both cold. And the neighbours have no need of a history lesson.'

And I pushed her inside and shut the door. But once Calypso started there wasn't any stopping her.

'The blood of all the races that occupied our land for thousands of years survived in the safety of those reeds.'

I put the kettle on, ignoring her.

'But when the ecosystem of life was disturbed, when they killed so many, everyone knew the land would not recover for a thousand years. It had taken so long to make and yet was broken in a moment.'

I shivered. The sky had darkened outside; the weather was closing in for the night. Calypso had started to pace up and down, her arms flailing wildly as she talked. The knocking on the other side of the wall continued. Aslam, I thought. Where the hell are you?

16.

Another blizzard arrived the next morning as promised. Was it our third or fourth? I had no idea. All I knew was that each one got worse. This time the whole country came to a standstill. Although a few flights were still going out of Gatwick, Hektor was stuck. Having dropped a customer off at the airport, he was stranded somewhere off the motorway. In the end he had to check himself into an expensive hotel because all the cheaper ones were full. He was livid. This new blizzard was meant to last for three days and, if the motorway didn't open, Hektor would soon be spending a fortune. But there were other more serious consequences. The blizzard had stopped the trains into the commercial centre of the city and so Lyle, who had a meeting with the lawyer in the morning, wasn't able to go to it. Calypso had been singing particularly loudly during the night and disloyally I had begun to sympathise with her neighbour. But I didn't dare ask her to stop even though I felt my head would burst. In the end, towards morning, I managed to persuade her to take a sleeping pill.

Then, at about ten o'clock, a woman from a local newspaper turned up on our doorstep. I had forgotten she had rung me a few days previously. She had sounded unusually sympathetic and I'd thought it might be a good idea to talk to her. Now she stood stamping the snow from her boots by the front door. Our breath came out in fistfuls of mist. Children were snapping off the icicles on the bushes outside. There was nothing for it but to invite the journalist in.

We looked at each other and liked what we saw. We must have been about the same age.

'God!' she said, stamping her feet more thoroughly on the rug inside the door. 'I haven't seen weather like this in years.'

Me neither.

The radiator in the hall wasn't working properly.

'My name is Sarah,' she said, holding out a cold hand to me. The sitting room was dark because of the still boarded-up windows. Small draughts of air made it impossible to stay there. There was a fan heater blowing in the kitchen so I invited her in there.

'I'm sorry about the mess,' I said. 'We're all … just …'

'Don't worry.'

I switched on the kettle while she settled herself at the kitchen table.

'Sorry,' I said again but she shook her head.

'It really doesn't matter. Where's your mother?'

I hesitated. Now that Calypso was asleep, I was loath to wake her. For all I knew, if she saw a journalist in the house she might take it upon herself to do something crazy like go out into the blizzard looking for Lyle. I didn't fancy chasing after her.

'It's okay,' Sarah said. 'I'll talk to you instead.'

I put a pot of fresh tea and a pint glass in front of her.

'What happened to the windows?'

I told her about the bricks.

'That's shocking,' she said.

When I didn't look surprised she raised an eyebrow.

'You don't think so?'

I didn't know what she meant.

'I mean you don't look shocked.'

I laughed.

'My shock levels have stabilised,' I said.

She was silent.

'This is a house under siege.'

And then the anger that I was suppressing began escaping like poison gas.

'If I tell you that I don't believe Aslam's done anything wrong would you believe me?'

'Of course. That's why I'm here. I want to write a piece from your point of view. Help me to do this.'

I hesitated. Then I began to talk.

'What is being said … this business of fanboys and radicalisation, about him being part of a British group helping the Desert Death Squad … this isn't true,' I said lamely. It was difficult to put into words the enormity of what we were facing. 'I mean, I know that he struggled to understand why these men are behaving in this way; he's interested in what they are doing because it affects all of us, but he's never *liked* what they are doing. He wanted to understand the psychology behind their behaviour, not dismiss it in the way politicians are doing. I mean, he's studying psychology for God's sake! Perhaps … he's being naïve, but a criminal, no.'

I stopped speaking. There was a sound of something sliding down from the roof. I jumped, thinking it was another brick, but it was only the snow falling away in great lumps, fooling us into believing the weather was improving.

'And the stuff they found on his computer?'

What stuff? *What stuff* for fuck's sake? Sarah shook her head and sipped her tea. I stared at her, the panic rising.

'You don't know?'

'No. Tell me.'

'He's been recruiting brides.'

I swallowed.

'*Aslam?*'

Oh no, I thought.

'You think so?'

'Apparently. That's what's being said in some of the more right-wing papers.'

No. It wasn't true. It was a lie. I *knew* it was. Sarah was looking at me sympathetically. Had she gone too far? her eyes said. We were both suddenly silenced.

'Is that what you think?' I asked at last.

'No. I don't think anything. You see … I know him too.'

She hesitated.

'I know you too; we've passed each other in the road. I'm a neighbour of Raphael's …'

Oh God, of course, I thought. *Of course!* It was that woman you'd told me about, Raphael. Remember? I glanced nervously towards the door.

'Look, could we stick to … I …'

'Of course, yes. I just wanted to identify myself. I'm not exactly a disinterested party. And I wanted you to know you can trust me – that's why I mentioned …'

'Yes, I understand. Thank you.'

I could hear movement in the room upstairs and then the sound of the toilet being flushed. Calypso was awake.

'Here she comes,' I said. 'You'd better talk to her. Just be careful, she's very fragile.'

From the way Calypso walked in, I could see she was going to be tricky.

'I'm not sick,' she announced.

Sarah smiled and stood up.

'Let me tell you something,' Calypso said, ignoring the outstretched hand. 'I've been listening to you. I hear everything. My son is not guilty of anything. All my son did was try to have a discussion online.'

'You don't know this,' I said.

Why was she saying this nonsense?

'He did write on the internet,' Calypso insisted. 'I told the police. I said, take his computer if you want. I don't care. Aslam doesn't care. He is innocent.'

I groaned inwardly. Would nothing save Aslam? Four men had been beheaded in the most terrible way on the London streets. Four other men were being held as hostages, somewhere. Why couldn't Calypso keep her big mouth shut? We none of us knew for *sure* if Aslam was innocent. And for all her friendliness, this woman was a journalist. She could write just about anything she wanted. I felt like hitting my mother.

'You journalists know *nothing*. Do you know my son? No, of course not. Yet already the world says he's guilty. Why else did they throw these bricks?'

I clenched my fists. Calypso was getting into her stride.

'Why do people need to throw bricks through our windows? What's the panic? Who's making them hate us? The government, the journalists, the police? First, you have two opposite sides. And after that you'll have another war.'

Oh, *right*! I thought. This is going really well. Thanks Lyle, thanks Calypso and Hektor stuck in your posh hotel. Calypso paused to draw breath. I thought she was going to have one of her asthma attacks. Alarmed, I stood up. Christ, my mother was a pain.

'You okay?'

I went in search of her inhaler and found the police had removed that, too.

'No one listened,' she shouted, trying to control her breathing at the same time.

'Shall I take your repeat prescription to the chemist?' I asked.

Calypso shook my head. The prescription had gone along with all the documents in the top drawer of her dressing table. I made a small sound of fury and Sarah continued to scribble away furiously.

'Would you like me to drive you to your doctor?' she asked eventually.

Calypso shook her head and, putting on her coat, she went outside to get her breath back. The frozen air, she told us, was unusually clean and would help her to do this. She would not be dissuaded.

'She's plucky,' Sarah said, watching her go.

Then she, too, stood up.

'Thank you,' she said. 'I think I have my story.'

17.

I *was* worried. No doubt about this. Of course I wouldn't dare say anything to the others, even Lyle. And certainly Calypso couldn't get a whiff of anything, God forbid. Her mind was like a pressure cooker at the moment; I wasn't going to undo the valve. But now after this many days, when I hadn't been thinking guiltily about you, Raphael, I'd been thinking guiltily about Aslam. And I kept asking myself, had he been up to some awful thing?

Which reminded me of something else. Two or three days before the police raid, during that last phone conversation we had, he'd said another really weird thing, which I'd forgotten until now. He told me that he and his best friend, Dolon, wanted to go back to our parents' birthplace.

'What the hell for?' I'd asked, shocked.

Aslam just shrugged.

'Why not? It's the Venice of the Middle East, isn't it? You'd go to Venice, wouldn't you? Given half a chance?'

He was talking as if going back to that shit-heap of bombs and beheadings was the most natural thing in the world.

'Aslam,' I'd screamed. 'There's a fucking war on there. Have you forgotten? You bloody idiot!'

Aslam laughed.

'You need to clean up your language, little sis,' was all he said.

And it was that sentence that had set alarm bells ringing in my head. What did he mean, clean up *my* language? Aslam swore like a trooper himself.

'That's different,' he said. 'I'm a man.'

I was silent. *What?* Was he really becoming like Hektor? With his mantra of a-woman's-place-is-behind-a-veil-with-her-mouth-shut-and-her-eyes-lowered? The same as our dad's?

I reminded him how we two had fought our parents for our freedom. How I used to run away screaming because Hektor wanted me to cover up and how only Lyle could make me come back home again. Had he forgotten how he had defended me and how our entire lives to date had been a struggle to live as we pleased and not according to what Hektor wanted? I stared at my brother.

Aslam laughed.

'How many times ...' I spluttered, angrily. 'It was *you* who said our culture had gone from the Middle Ages to the twenty-first century in a few decades. Have you forgotten? You said people hadn't had time to adjust to the change. *You* said our people still had this absurd mentality, unlike the people in the West, who'd changed slowly over centuries. My God, Aslam, are you now talking like a medieval man yourself?'

I was really very angry but Aslam was looking at me lazily.

'Let me give you some advice,' he said, finally. 'I know you're seeing some man and I know he isn't one of ours. You need to stop trying so hard to be a Western person. You need to clean up your act.'

There was a pause while I looked at him in disbelief.

'The world we are living in is changing, little sis.'

'Stop calling me "little sis",' I snapped.

Aslam held his hand up.

'For your own protection, sis,' he said. 'I would cover up … Oh and, by the way, are you still a virgin?'

I was speechless. Was he joking?

'My own protection?' I asked nastily. 'What you mean, against the weather?'

My brother looked at me expressionlessly. Then he picked up his jacket.

'I'm off,' he said. 'I'll see you at Mum's on Friday. Dolon and his mother will be there.'

He gave me a kiss. Then he hesitated and tapped me on the cheek.

'You can bring the boyfriend if you like,' he teased.

'I haven't got a boyfriend,' I shouted, but he was already out of the door and didn't hear me.

That was the extent of the conversation we'd had. It had seemed ghastly at the time, I still worried about it but I was not going to let my imagination run away with me, I thought firmly. No. I would wait. And be calm. We couldn't all have hysterics, could we?

18.

Nothing much happened in the next few days. The blizzard stopped for a few hours and a heavy white mist swallowed up the trunks of the trees. Conditions were worsening by the hour. In the end Lyle did manage to get to his appointment and we heard, via the lawyer that a conversation was taking place with the Home Office and New Scotland Yard. But we still had no idea where Aslam was being held, still no word from the authorities. Our requests had now been put in writing to the Home Office and a reply had arrived. Just a single sentence: 'Your request is being processed and you will hear shortly.' This was followed by a serial number that we were asked to keep in a safe place. I had no illusions. Since most of the government offices were functioning with a skeleton staff, further information wasn't going to come quickly. Phone calls were a waste of time; all you got from a phone call was an automated voice. However, one good thing had happened. Sarah, the journalist, had written a brilliant piece that appeared in one of the more progressive newspapers. It had been written from my point of view, was very complimentary towards me and also towards Calypso. As a result we got a call from a radio station asking if I would like to speak on a live programme. However, Lyle and the lawyer were not happy about this.

'Wait until we get news about his whereabouts,' they advised.

The radio station was happy to shelve my appearance for a week.

'By then,' Lyle said, 'we should have heard from Aslam.'

Meanwhile the weather remained truly appalling. The wind had started coming in hard from Siberia. It blew drifts of snow across the roads, taking with it the wheelie bins and supermarket trolleys and bicycles. And no sooner had the snow hit the ground than it froze. The council put salt on the main roads and people dug their cars out of the side streets. But as fast as they did so, the snow returned to destroy their work with effortless ease. Winter, like terror, had infiltrated the white city. It was here to stay. It mocked and hounded us, it howled around the chimneys and it rattled through the tower blocks. We meant nothing to the weather. In the days that followed Sarah's visit, I did nothing except look online at the newspaper. Thank God I could still access the internet on my phone. On the following Monday the snow eased slightly and Hektor returned. Several days of staying in an expensive hotel by the airport had done nothing to improve his temper so, unable to stand his complaints or Calypso's singing, I decided to attempt the journey back to my place on the bus. At least I could get a change of clothes, get warm, see you, Raphael, breathe a little easier. But the bus broke down and in the end I walked back to Railton Road in the frozen dark. Mission unaccomplished.

Hektor went back to work. The demand for taxis was so great that despite the suspicious glances of the other drivers his boss was pleased to see him. I must say, Calypso and I were glad to have him gone. As my mother clearly wasn't about to do anything about the state of the house, I decided to give the whole place a deep clean. It was the only way to stop myself from going mad. I began by sorting out the mess left by the police. And so our second week passed. By now it was impossible to remember what life had been like just a short time ago. Lyle, too, had changed. He had become silent, spent most of his days on the phone and came over faithfully every night. He'd had no luck in getting any news. Aslam had literally vanished into thin air and another appeal to a High Court judge demanding information had been lodged.

Then Iris, who hadn't visited us for days, came over. Aslam had spent a lot of time at Iris's house when he was growing up. He and her sons, especially Dolon, were close, yet none of the boys had visited us since Aslam had been arrested. So I was glad to see Iris that day. Perhaps she would cheer Calypso up a little.

But Iris hadn't braved the snow to cheer anyone up. She was in a terrible state.

'They came for Dolon too,' she cried.

Dolon. Aslam's closest friend.

'They wanted him for questioning.'

We stared at her, aghast.

It seemed the police had come for Dolon the night before. They had kept him for hours and finally let him go at midnight. He was shaken, refusing to talk and was, at this point, still in bed with the door locked. Iris was afraid the police would be back. The whole of Hurst Street had been raided and five other boys, all known to Dolon, had also been arrested.

'They can do whatever they like now,' Iris said.

She wrung her hands. Her husband had wanted them to

leave the country but where could they go?

'At our age,' she cried. 'We can't start again. This is our home. It has been our home for more than forty years. We might as well die as leave this place.'

She was crying inconsolably.

'I am frightened,' she whispered. And then she asked: 'Still no news about Aslam?'

I shook my head and at that Calypso went properly berserk.

No one was doing anything, she cried, no one cared about her son. Everyone was useless. When I pointed out that Lyle was doing the best he could, but that the weather had been hampering all his efforts, she threw a saucepan across the room. Huge tears rolled down her face. She began to rock and inevitably the singing started up again in earnest. Iris stared at her in horror. Not having seen Calypso for almost a week she was taken aback by the change. I suspected that, although Iris probably blamed Aslam for what was happening and had come here to say so, she was so shocked by the change in Calypso she wouldn't now say anything.

I made tea and we talked about the boys. Iris's husband had gone to speak to their lawyer.

'He is terrified that Dolon is involved in something bad.'

Iris herself could not believe her son would do wrong.

'He studies politics. It doesn't mean he's dabbling in it,' she said. 'If only we'd found these boys wives none of this would have happened.'

Calypso snorted angrily.

'Drink your tea,' I said and we sat in silence, sipping the sweet, honey-coloured liquid.

'Have they done the windows yet?' Iris asked after a while, calming down slightly.

'Yes, yesterday.'

'And nothing more has happened?'

'Not so far. There is another story in the news at the moment so everyone's attention is diverted.'

She nodded. Yes, she knew. At least this murder wasn't anything to do with us.

I wished I could pray; I wished I had a God of my own who could provide for me. But I hadn't and it was too late to go looking for one now. As Iris and Calypso were busy talking to each other in Arabic I decided, in order not to go crazy, that I would leave them for a bit. I went into the hall and put my coat and boots on. Then I closed the front door softly and slipped away towards the towpath.

To my left was the great Victorian park that bordered the canal. I quickened my pace. The snow-light was dazzling on the thin, drooping willow branches. The landscape stretched before me like a painting – the dark-green hedges, the cluster of bare trees, a few black birds against all the whiteness. Yes, this treacherous landscape *was* lovely. I glanced at my watch. It was a quarter past three. If I was quick I could walk through the park towards your house, Raphael. I wouldn't have long – I'd promised Lyle I would stay with my mother until he got back at five – but at least I could see you, however briefly. Crossing the road, I headed in the direction of your house.

By the time I arrived at the top of the main road that led to the turning into your street, the sky was looking thundery again. Just five more minutes and I would be there. I passed the Post Office. There was an empty pushchair with a dog attached to it, who was whining. I walked on and came to the café on the corner of your street, but to my amazement it was boarded up. What? I thought, shocked. How could this have happened? The whole place had an abandoned air about it. Pausing, I tried to peer in through the nailed-up boards. I could see nothing. A passer-by eyed me suspiciously and I turned the corner hurriedly. Although our photographs hadn't appeared in any paper, still, you never knew who might recognise me. A moment later I arrived at your house. But although I knocked and knocked there was no answer.

'Raphael!' I shouted through the letterbox. 'It's me, Hera.'

Still nothing. I walked around to your back gate but it was locked. So I knocked on it, although I knew that if you were in your shed with the fan heater blowing you would probably not hear me. Cursing, I glanced at my watch. I was running out of time. I hadn't thought to bring a pen or any paper, so I couldn't even write a note. There wasn't anything I could do but turn back uneasily and head towards home. And then at the corner, sitting on a snow-covered low wall, was the cat.

'Hello, Cretino,' I said stroking it. 'Where's your owner then?'

The cat purred and rubbed itself against me. It didn't look particularly hungry. At least, I reassured myself, you must be around feeding it or it would have meowed when it saw me.

When I returned home, as soon as I stepped into the house, I knew something was wrong. Lyle was waiting for me.

'Where's Calypso?' I asked.

I didn't look at him. I was feeling guilty that I had left my post.

'She's at Iris's house. She's left a note for you,' Lyle said.

There was something in his voice that was not right. I waited.

'What is it?' I asked at last.

Lyle was staring at me. Somewhere in the distance an

19.

I stared at Lyle. He was crying. I don't think I had ever seen a grown man cry until now. Aslam?

'What's happened?'

Lyle shook his head.

'For God's sake, Lyle!' I screamed.

The door was still open. The snow had started up again, a few flakes floating lazily in the still air. Lyle reached into his bag.

The bundle took my breath away. It was torn and bloodstained and stank and I shrank away from it. We were both crying now. Aslam's clothes, the beautiful green shirt with tropical birds on it, torn to shreds. His trainers with the knots still done up, his socks, his jeans with dried blood all over the crotch. Oh my God. Held together by string. What had they done to my brother? Lyle shook his head, embracing me as no man from our culture did. I started to sob.

'He's dead,' I said.

It wasn't a question.

'No.' Lyle shook his head.

'What then?'

The clothes had fallen onto the floor and Lyle bent to pick them up.

'Tell me!' I screamed.

Slowly he straightened up. When he spoke, his voice was indistinct and choked and I leaned forward. But I *still* could not understand. In the last few moments the snow had quickened. Flakes like clumps of fur were being torn from the sky as Lyle told me what had happened to my brother.

They had taken Aslam away in the night, but which night he did not know. They would not tell either the lawyer or Lyle where he was. When they'd handed over his clothes and asked him to sign for them, Lyle had broken down, thinking, as I had, that Aslam had died in custody. But they had assured him that this was not so. Aslam was wearing prison clothes.

'But which prison is he in?' the lawyer had shouted. 'You have to tell me. I am representing him. You *have* to tell me. It is the *law!*'

The police officer had stared impassively, very calm, very cold.

'A letter will be sent to you shortly. Until we have clearance from the Home Office we cannot divulge his whereabouts.'

Lyle had demanded to speak to the person in charge but that man *was* the person in charge. Eventually, realising they were getting nowhere, the lawyer had persuaded Lyle to leave the security headquarters. The lawyer went off to make more phone calls and Lyle wandered around for a bit, aimlessly clutching Aslam's belongings. He did not want to come to see us with just the clothes. He went into a café and ordered some tea. At last the lawyer rang him.

'Go home,' he said. 'I've contacted the MP and Amnesty. I've talked to the Mayor and the Home Office, too. And I've found out what's happened.'

It was how Lyle got the information he wanted. It hadn't been easy but a loophole, Article F36/a17, invoked an old law that gave a lawyer the right to know where his client was being held. That loophole, Lyle told me, would soon be closed. The lawyer had been passed from one department to another until finally he was summoned to the office of a man whose name was withheld.

The man was from Counter Terrorism. Dressed in a dark suit, the man smiled. It was simply a facial movement. There was nothing human behind it.

'Aslam is being deported,' Lyle told me slowly. 'Today.'

'Deported?' I asked wonderingly. 'But he was born here; where is he being deported to?'

Lyle shook his head. He cried harder.

'When?'

'He would not say but I have my ...'

He broke off. I stared at him in disbelief. Shock. Open-mouthed shock, hands raised. Shock, like death, nearly always arrives with a look of surprise. Shock has its own set rules.

'No!'

'Yes!'

'But where?'

'The Arena.'

Lyle would not look at me. Hell in an orange jumpsuit, was that it?

'They *told* you?'

'No. Amnesty told me.'

Speechlessly I kept staring at the bundle in my hands.

'The blood ...' I whispered.

'But he is alive,' Lyle said. 'Otherwise they wouldn't be taking him anywhere. Think about it.'

I thought about it. I couldn't get very far with my thoughts. What should we do next?

'Amnesty is going to the airport. They are trying to get a special injunction to stop them dragging him onto that plane. And if not, I swear to you I'm going out there too to bring him home. But first we're going to try to stop them taking him.'

My mouth was dry. Tears spilled from my eyes. How could he stop anything this government wanted to do? Where would the money come from to take him to the Arena?

Suddenly, Lyle's mobile went off and he searched frantically for it while I watched helplessly.

'What? When?'

There was a pause and the next moment he was galvanised into action.

'Yes, *yes*, will do. *Now!* I'll call you back.'

'*What?*' I asked but he was already opening up his laptop.

'Now,' Lyle said. '*Now*. He's at the airport. We can watch the flight live – oh my God, my God! They couldn't get the injunction.'

Horrified, I watched as he tried to connect to the internet. The small wheel turned round and round on his screen. Was his computer going to crash? Finally, after an agony of silence, he managed to find the website for the airline and began frantically searching for live flight tracking. He typed in the number of the flight as I watched an image of a plane appear on the screen. There was a countdown device clicking away the minutes. Lyle's phone rang again.

'Yes, yes, I have, I have.'

'What is it, Lyle?' I asked, desperate.

'They're taking him to the plane. He's handcuffed, he's kicking up a fuss.'

'Why the fuck don't you guys do something!' I screamed.

'Do fucking something, don't just watch a computer screen.'

But it was too late. He had been given the information too late for anything. These people had thought of *everything*. Nothing was going to stop them now. The minutes ticked on. I could hear the voice on the other end of the phone talking.

'They're dragging him now. Four security guards.'

Four? For one slight boy? Who were these brutes?

'Oh my God!'

'Fucking hell! What is this place that we live in?'

It was too late. He was already gone from us, already out of reach. I turned away and began vomiting as Lyle continued to cry in harsh, dry sobs.

'I will find him,' he vowed, his voice broken. 'I will go to the ends of the earth if need be, I will turn every stone, however long it takes, and I will bring him back.'

I thought of the Arena. A place of such immense fear and loathing, so far away, so inaccessible, so desperately inhuman. There have been many cruel prisons in the world. But the two that stand out are Hitler's camps and the Arena.

We were both crying helplessly. The image of the plane began to move slightly. It began taxiing slowly down the runway.

'Three flights away, that's all,' Lyle kept saying. 'I shall get there. I'm getting the permits by tomorrow. We have contacts; we'll get help from abroad. Trust me. My son, oh my son!'

I was crying so hard that I didn't register his words. Not then, not for several hours. All I could think of was Aslam, my brother, all alone, with no family, beaten, frightened, not knowing what further horrors awaited him. And I thought of us all and what this would do to us and how we would cope, living in a country that was our home though the word no longer had any meaning. I thought of the sky and the birds that would be in the place where the Arena was, flying freely with no intervention from man and, as I continued to weep, I saw Lyle turn towards the doorway with a terrified look on his face. For both of us had forgotten about Calypso, who stood soaking wet from the blizzard, watching us with a question on her face. Outside the sun was setting in an icy wintry sky.

20.

Calypso had collapsed in the doorway and the ambulance took ten minutes to arrive. Given the terrible weather and the huge cuts to the emergency services I suppose that was quick. But I could not find her identity card without which nothing was possible. The police had removed everything.

'I don't think they had any insurance,' Lyle whispered.

He was pale and was sweating slightly.

'I remember Hektor saying it was one of the things he had to do.'

For a moment the paramedics hesitated. It was against the law for them to treat a patient if there was no evidence of insurance. I searched through the filing cabinet, frantically throwing things on the ground, while Lyle pleaded with the men to help Calypso. He was crying and explaining about the police raid and our documents. He was speaking in broken English now, stumbling over his words, tears streaming down his face.

'Please,' he begged. 'Please don't let her die.'

The paramedic was a man in his fifties. I could only suppose that he remembered the kind of emergency service we used to have before each consecutive government destroyed our health service.

'She's my mother,' I said.

And now I was choking. The paramedic looked from Lyle to me. I found Calypso's identity card, held it out to him and he made his decision.

Calypso was given immediate cardiopulmonary resuscitation and put into the ambulance meant for other, richer women. Then we were speeding across the frozen city, past houses knee-deep in layers of snow, with grief howling along that suburban road.

'I know a hospital where they will treat her no matter what,' the paramedic said, lights flashing, slicing through my tears. Lyle was following the tail lights of the ambulance in his car, struggling to keep up. We sped across the empty dual carriageway. Above us an aeroplane blinked a blood-red light as it left the city. The plane carrying a shackled Aslam was somewhere out over the Atlantic while I alone sat beside our mother.

I wonder if things can happen too early or too late, or if in fact everything happens at exactly the right time. The sky had turned the colour of a peach. It was diffused and soft. The snow was still falling and the visibility was so bad that the driver had to slow down. I did not know that I was sobbing uncontrollably. The hospital was approaching but the activity inside the ambulance seemed to increase.

'One minute more. Hold on for just one minute longer.'

'Is she going to be all right?'

The paramedic was too busy to answer but the nurse murmured something I couldn't quite catch.

'Oh God! Oh God!' I whispered.

Over and over again I was praying to a God I did not have.

'Please, no!'

The headlights from Lyle's car shone faintly behind us. The paramedic was speaking on the phone and I heard the line crackle and break up. Then the monitor overhead began to flicker too as the power started to fail again.

'What's happening?' I asked in a panic of despair.

No one answered. The lights flickered once more. It came on and went off again and then the monitor, uttering one single and continuous wail, blanked out.

'I'm sorry, love,' the paramedic said, his arm going around me. 'I'm *so* sorry, love, but your mum has just died.'

Outside, the snow swirled furiously in the frozen air. It lifted the branches, shaking them so that the dark birds rose like a cloud of black smoke in the otherwise white air.

How strange life is with its frayed edges and last chances.

Everything slowed down and I saw footsteps in the snow. Lyle leaping out like a fawn from his car, crying into the whiteness. Would my mother have been saved if she had had insurance? Would she have reached a hospital sooner? 'I'm sorry, love, your mum has just died' are words that will for ever be etched on my heart. Do you know what those words mean to me? I wanted to scream. Do you know about my brother who is flying above us in a steel container at this very moment, who *loves* our mother, yet does not know she is dead? Do you know about Hektor, the taxi driver, lover of a dead woman who did not love him? Do you know of the young fawn she called Lyle?

I could hear the future getting into position like a dancer on a stage before the curtain goes up.

We buried Calypso at dawn. She was swathed in white, covered from head to foot, strangely small. A precious bundle that was about to be discarded in a pit of snow and earth. One toe jutted out. A toe whose bone would soon be picked clean, turned calcium-white as a star. There was snow everywhere. Imagine it. Hektor and the imam reciting the Qur'an, words from my lost childhood in an English-Muslim grave. Dark against white. A hole in a wide space. A cluster of people, their heads bowed. This is the day of my mother's funeral, I thought, trying and failing to give the words some sense. And Lyle, a thin man in black, leaning against some other tombstone like a Victorian mourner, complete with distraught look, no longer strong, all lost, broken. Thinking, what was *he* thinking on this day of two lost loves?

Beside him stood Iris, one of her sons, whose name escapes me (not Dolon, of course; he was on another plane skywards to hell), and Sarah, the journalist, hand on my arm. The neighbours – *the neighbours?* Well, death, they say, is a great leveller. We had been blinded by snow for so long we could scarcely tell the difference between that and being blinded by grief. I listened to the imam and was not comforted.

But then someone said:

'Every moment is a beginning and an end.'

'Raphael, I need you now,' I said out loud.

21.

By the time I came to you, Raphael, I was already paralysed by grief. I came through a snowstorm of unrelenting despair, my hands cold as the turned earth on my mother's grave, a blind mole swathed in black hurrying across the white park. That was how I came. Running towards you, carrying this weight in my heart. I barely noticed the sky filling with seagulls driven inland by the rough seas. They floated white against the white landscape, rising and falling like paper kites tossed in an invisible wind. The air splintered as though a prism had been placed before my eyes.

'*Raphael,*' was all I could say.

My breath came out in gasps. I had no strength left.

'*Como estás, querida?*'

From the interior of the house the light fell with distant softness on your face.

'*Ishtar?*'

I shook my head, mute. Comprehension was beyond me.

'What is it, darling?'

My heart rolled itself into a stone ball and travelled down into the pit of my stomach and then, in a moment of monstrous agony, I felt tears spurt out of my eyes. And I was falling.

'*Ven, querida.* Come, darling.'

I shook my head again, confused. In your kitchen you placed me on a chair like a sick child and wiped my eyes and kept on wiping them because the tears would not stop falling no matter what you said. And in the stillness of this iced-up, snowbound, bitter world I told you first, haltingly, about my brother.

'*Querida, querida,*' you said. 'My Ishtar, don't cry.'

You had turned pale.

'*Disappeared?*' you asked. 'Did you say your brother has *disappeared?*'

I nodded, too choked to speak. I was beyond repair. You looked over your shoulder as if there was someone else in the room witnessing this. The clock ticked, uncaring.

'I told you,' you burst out, 'I *told* you this would happen again.'

Somewhere high above the snow clouds and the darkness, we could hear a plane flying over the city. We listened until the sound faded to nothing and then we turned to each other.

When I spoke of Calypso it was with a different grief but spoken in the same voice. Hearts, I told you, could be broken many times. There was no warmth, no light, no stars, no hope. Only the snow continuing to fall with steady disregard for any of us.

'There is only you now,' I said. 'The others have gone.'

You looked at me gravely and shook your head.

'I can live with that,' I said, crying. 'Somehow if I have you that is enough.'

Still you said nothing. Disbelief stood between us.

'I'm telling you,' I said fiercely. 'With you I will survive.'

The room seemed to grow darker, as though all the sad

light of the last few hours had taken refuge in us. Your face was caught in deep shadows as you listened but still you could not speak. With an awful cry I raised my arms and, as I did so, I caught a glimpse of your face opening up at last. You looked stunned and a moment later you began to kiss me.

'I am here now,' you murmured, 'you must not cry. I cannot bear it.'

But I was crying in earnest and so you held me, murmuring softly. Words I could not understand.

'*Querida*,' you said. 'Why were you so long in coming? I have waited years and years, you know.'

And when I didn't answer:

'How could you be so cruel to me?'

Time unfolded without notification. There were ghosts in the room but I don't remember where they came from or what they wanted from us. All I cared about was the hands touching mine, the lips on my throat, the corners of my mouth kissed – at last. Skin on skin. My thoughts were confused; there were words half forming. No more veils. At last! And all the time, try as we could to banish them, the ghosts pressed closer.

'*Raphael*,' I said, in this new voice I was learning to acknowledge as my own. Desire and the breathlessness of grief snared me further, but you only held me closer. No words, not now. Words were for later. So I kissed you back, fearlessly, and the last taboo, along with my past, was broken.

Instinct kept me still after that. In the shabby room with no blinds, with the cold seeping through the corners of the window frame, in the narrow bed I had never seen until now, with your calloused hands gentle against the clothes you were peeling off me, I discovered that I had been right all along.

Yes, you wanted me. All those months of holding back had been useless. I was triumphant. Surely my mother would have been happy for me now? A strange, calming effect descended on my half-awake senses, spinning and breaking into a slow, beautiful beginning. You waited, then waited some more, until the stone knot in my heart had begun to melt. And when you could no longer wait you flooded me as though all the years of your life had been saved for this moment.

At last, after months of snow and freezing ice, the wind seemed to drop. For minutes on end there was only silence. We listened to it, astonished.

'Spring?' you murmured, your voice surprised. 'Could it be?'

When I opened my eyes you were looking at me gravely and I knew without a shadow of a doubt that from now on I would forever be defined by your eyes.

'All the stars are out,' I heard you say. 'Every single one, Ishtar; did you know?'

Then you propped yourself up and looked down at me as though you were trying to memorise my face. Your eyes were the colour of the deepest, darkest, unfathomable water. You are mine now, I thought, but when I traced your scars with the tips of my fingers, you winced.

'Don't,' you said, your voice suddenly harsh, breaking some invisible spell that held us both in its grip.

The cat jumped up onto the covers and we realised that we were both cold. You got up to put another log on the fire. I watched you go. I sensed you did not want me to see how thin you were.

'Why have you turned that photograph to the wall?' I asked.

You were silent, your face turned slightly away, and with a shock I saw that *you* were crying. All morning I had watched men cry but these reluctantly wrenched-up sobs were different.

'What is it?' I asked but you only shook your head.

Again and again.

'I love you,' I said.

Suddenly I saw that it was not just objects that had shadows on them; events did too.

We were still hungry for each other.

'I love you, too,' you replied, your limbs stretched over mine, love stirring in you.

But I sensed that something had begun to move you away from me.

Afterwards you looked at me with infinite sadness.

'You cannot explain love,' you said as though in answer to a question I had asked. 'That's how it gets ruined.'

I disagreed, hotly. Ghosts or no ghosts, we had made a promise to each other, hadn't we?

'The world is a falling pack of cards,' you insisted. 'And the closer to extinction it gets the faster and harder the force of the fall.'

I began crying again. 'Don't! Don't spoil things.'

What I had lost was surfacing to claim me. Dimly I understood that, whichever way I turned, I would still have to face this fact.

'Tell me your story, Raphael,' I pleaded, instead. 'Please.'

There was a scar inside you that had begun to break and bleed and for the first time I was afraid.

Much later, after you told me, finally, you stirred. I was speechless.

'I'm sorry. I've done it all wrong,' you said, eventually, looking ashamed. 'I meant to distract you but I have hurt you more.'

'No,' I told you, covering your lips with mine.

But the truth was I felt that really you were speaking to the stars, to the snow, to the cold; to anything except me. Confused, I moved restlessly.

'I have to go back home,' I said, in a small voice. 'Hektor might need me, Lyle too. There might be news of Aslam …'

My voice trailed off. Hopelessness engulfed me. We were both shipwrecked.

When I was dressed, you took me in your arms and held me.

'Remember,' you said, 'we will all die in a war that holds no meaning for any of us. That's how stupid we are.'

But when I began to speak, you buried your face in my hair.

Outside the wind had picked up again. Another blizzard was starting up. I began to cry. I cried differently, as if for the first time. That was when you told me about the oldest war of all.

'The Trojan War,' you said. 'What did that achieve? It established no boundaries, won no territories and furthered no causes.'

I cried harder.

'Go home, darling,' you said in English. 'Go home to your father. Tomorrow is time enough for us.'

I

Before the beginning of the Reign of Terror he had been called *Doctor* Raphael Kalchas and in the city where he lived, known locally as Santiopolis, eyewitnesses had reported sightings of a rare bird of prey. The bird had never been seen in that area before. It was almost completely white with black feet and a red crest and it was presumed to have strayed down from the high mountains whose eternally snow-covered peaks were believed to be its natural habitat. In fact this was not the case and the bird had come from another part of the world entirely, one not known to the people living on the brink of the Reign of Terror.

When Dr Kalchas first heard of these sightings he became both excited and frightened. His childhood had left a residue of superstition like a trail of desert salt across his life. A bird of prey outside its natural habitat was odd. Nevertheless, he rushed home across the rough desert plain, his body dripping with salty sweat, his eyes half closed by the dazzle, to see if it was indeed true that such a bird existed. Until that moment he believed the creature was just a mythical being.

The bird had flown eastwards towards the long ridge of high arid mountains. It glided and tilted into the sun before disappearing into some secret wild part of the desert. Dr

Kalchas looked through his binoculars until they misted over and until the bird was simply a small dark shape merging into the sun. Then he went home. He was disappointed. He was convinced the bird had come from the sea, or at least from somewhere where there was water. It was winter so he assumed it had travelled from a colder place, perhaps the high mountains, or even further. But he had never heard of a bird that could travel this far, unless of course it was one of those vultures that came occasionally to this stark landscape.

The next time he saw it was at dusk in that brief moment before darkness fell and the stars appeared. There was simply a harsh call and suddenly it was before him; eyes hooded, fearlessly approaching him across open ground with a steady wingbeat. Dr Kalchas was stunned, rooted to the spot, caught in the magic of such a flight. For a moment he thought he was about to be attacked but then with another cry the bird lifted smoothly and flew over him. So close that its wings created a slight breeze that ruffled Raphael Kalchas's hair. He decided he had to make friends with this bird.

Afterwards he was amused by the uselessness of his chosen task. No wild bird would allow itself to be tamed by an amateur like himself. When he told them at home what he was planning they shook their heads.

'Don't,' his mother told him. 'You have a new life beginning. Don't go near it. It is a bird of warning; it's come like the comet that appeared in the sky last month.'

His wife, too, was upset. There was a spool of fear in her eyes. 'They are not normal birds,' she said, shivering. 'They are like humans.'

He laughed. Didn't she know the difference between a bird of prey and a human?

'Birds kill only when they are hungry,' he told his wife. Unlike humans.

'*We* are the killers,' his wife said. 'We stink of death. Your mother is right. That bird is some sort of messenger; keep away from it.'

'I told you,' he said. 'It's just a bird, for God's sake. It sees like a Cubist painter sees, in planes and shapes and form rather than detail. It's a wonderful thing! How can it be bad?'

But secretly he, too, felt a little uneasy in the face of all this superstition.

For the next few days he began to track its flight: wings hanging loosely as it glided, drooping shoulders before suddenly swooping down, camouflaged so well against the dry red earth. When it rose again it shook its prey like a dog shaking dirt from his body. Then it climbed steeply into the slight east wind, turned abruptly and headed south. Kalchas didn't see it again for some time. But later, as he was returning home on foot, he found a small carcass, neck broken, an untouched breast, the jagged ends of bone. Only the eyes of that small animal had been left; still very lovely and with the shine of a life recently over. Raphael Kalchas felt an infinite sadness come over him. Perhaps his wife and his mother had been right and there was something deeply unpleasant about these birds. As he stood looking at the dead animal he heard it make its harsh screeching distinctive sound.

Kreek, kreek.

Looking up, he saw it suspended in the twilight, sepulchral and ghostly, and instantly he forgot everything except its magnificent beauty.

When he returned home he tried describing what he'd felt but his wife wasn't interested. There was no one he could tell about this inexplicable fascination.

'I hope nothing bad will happen,' was all his mother said, disapprovingly. 'There's been some odd things taking place recently.'

'Like what?'

His mother shook her head and Raphael Kalchas sighed. He loved his family but they were simple people. He decided to keep his sightings of the bird to himself.

II

From the town the land flowed like a river of sand and stones bending around the north side of the ridge. Beyond it, the upper valley was a flat open expanse of space with no protection from the fierce sunlight. No one ventured to this part of the desert. It was the driest spot on earth and it made the sky clear and unpolluted at night. From space the desert was a small strip of camel-coloured earth amidst the blue of the many oceans of the planet. But in reality it stretched for hundreds of miles, hot, treacherous and lonely. Dr Kalchas knew to respect it, never venturing out without water and a compass. He had lived in this area all his life apart from the brief spell he had spent in Adresteia, a town north of Santiopolis, at the university where he had studied astronomy. The stars were his life and, after that, his passion was for birds. Later, after he fell in love, the birds and the stars merged into one and the same thing. Love, he often said, had no boundaries.

After his doctorate Kalchas began working at a small government-sponsored observatory mapping the stars. In the decades since the Second World War nothing much had been learnt from it and few people were aware that another Reign of Terror, more localised but just as brutal, was about to begin. Kalchas understood that if war had taught civilisation anything it was only how to repeat unspeakable evil. The war and all its horror had set a new standard for other dictators following in the wake of Hitler.

In his journal on the day he had seen the bird he wrote: *War teaches the human animal nothing better than how to kill, maim and torture each other with greater imagination, greater ease and greater indifference.*

They had not been married long and his young wife worked as a freelance journalist for a small local newspaper. With his salary and her intermittent contributions they managed quite well. Their apartment was in a tenement block painted yellow and quite a few of their neighbours were their friends. They both loved their work but Raphael had to work long hours into the dawn. When his wife grumbled he smiled.

'Stars only come out at night, Ishtar!' he'd remind her.

His passion for the stars had begun when he was small, a child sandwiched between two brothers, called Ares and Achilles. His father had bought him a book on astronomy and the young Raphael had fallen in love with the idea that the star's incandescence emanated from thousands of light years away. He wanted to know more about the past from aeons ago. The universe became an obsession. Ishtar, when they first met, used to tease him, saying he was not content with a woman here on earth but wanted one in the sky, too.

Sometimes at work, if the boss wasn't present, Raphael Kalchas and the other astronomers would indulge in a little beverage to help them through the night. On his return at dawn, he would kiss Ishtar awake, and watch with amusement as she wrinkled her nose. It was the smell of the *chimarrao* that he had been drinking all night that she disliked.

'I need to keep awake, don't I?' he would tell her.

On the days when there was no excitement at work, which of course was most days, he would become tired.

'When you are happy,' he would say, 'thoughts aren't all that necessary. So you fall asleep unless you drink *chimarrao*!'

She would laugh then and accept this excuse. She accepted anything he told her, she said, because she loved him.

Their lives were simple with simple pleasures. One time they had gone away from the dust and the heat for a holiday. They had never had a proper holiday together. It was Raphael who decided the time had come for one.

'Where would you like to go?' he asked.

Although less demonstrative than she was, Raphael would do anything for her.

'The sea,' she told him.

There was no other place worth visiting. Mountains were no use. It was possible to see the mountains even from where they lived. So what was the point of getting closer to them?

'Sometimes you might find getting closer changes your perspective of things,' he had teased her.

But, no, she had shaken her head. It was the sea she longed for. The sea was like another species, a different life form. So they went to the sea and Ishtar found it was exactly as she had dreamed.

In the first moment of arrival at the shore, they were silenced by its vastness.

'Did you think,' she had asked him cautiously that night as they lay in the room they had rented, 'did you think it would be this big?'

He was lying on his back, naked, with his arm under her head, gazing at the stars.

'No,' he said, thinking how large the stars were and how bright the moon was.

'Are you surprised?' she asked.

Raphael was silent and the sea moved softly nearby.

'Moonlight takes a second to reach us,' he said at last. 'And sun and light somewhat longer.'

'How much longer?'

'About eight minutes.'

They sighed, humbled by nature, unable to detach themselves from the hiss and sigh of the waves. Their eyes were glued to the moonlight that lay in a long wide boulevard across the restless sea.

'Even if we lived for ever I wouldn't forget tonight,' she said, and when he said nothing she raised herself up on her elbow and added, seriously, 'I will remember tonight on my dying day!'

He had laughed, kissing her impatiently, and soon they were making love for the third time that night.

They slept until the dawn rose. It was a dawn so different from the dawn in the dust bowl where they had been brought up. Light spread across the sky. Seagulls appeared out of nowhere, their raucous cries drowning out the gentle sound of the sea. They dressed hurriedly like children and ran down to the beach – they *were* still children, he thought now – throwing themselves into the warm waters, laughing, swimming, splashing each other. And then, soon after, hunger overtook them, first for *pan amasado* with *manjar*, and soon after for each other.

'We shouldn't make love on a full stomach,' Ishtar said, seriously.

'Really?' he'd asked, pretending to look worried. 'But you know I can't stop now.'

'Well …' she said, frowning, 'perhaps just this once …' And then she had seen him laughing at her and she'd beat him with the palms of her hands, laughing too.

Afterwards, he remembered thinking how her hands had seemed like delicate fronds beating lightly on his back. Afterwards, long afterwards, even now, he still had this thought. Her touch like her voice had a habit of never quite leaving him.

They stayed beside the sea for another three days before returning home. And, when Helen was almost two, they came back one more time. One last time. They hadn't known it was the last time. Not then.

III

Raphael hadn't wanted a child until the coup had taken place. All he wanted was to live peacefully with Ishtar. But after the coup, overnight, life changed beyond recognition. After that first purge they would huddle together by the radio and listen to how the terrible events were unfolding in the news. They had both lost family members on the first day. It was just chance that neither of them had been on the streets at the time. At 7 a.m. on that fateful morning everyone who had been outside –men, women and even schoolchildren – had been rounded up and taken to the stadiums. Nothing more was heard of them.

The military kept the victims locked in the stadium for twelve hours. They shone fluorescent lights into the prisoners' eyes until they were blinded. They made them stand upright, next to strangers as well as people they knew well. From time to time some people were dragged away screaming, never to be seen again. Shots were fired and bodies piled on top of each other. The soldiers were young, mere children with guns. They spat on the people, blindfolded them, tied them up, and bundled others into trucks. Only a small handful escaped, released in order to spread the word, to tell those outside what had happened. Some days later, when Raphael and Ishtar had been frantically trying and failing to contact their parents, a friend came to see them.

'They played at killing me,' he wept. 'They shot me with blanks, then they dragged me into a room. I smelled of my own shit. They broke my arm in three places. And then, without warning, they released me.'

The friend had lost every member of his own family: his parents, his wife and his children. He had caught a glimpse of Raphael's father in the stadium, their eyes had met briefly, and a wordless message passed between them. That was why he was here, to give Raphael the unspoken message of what had been done. The only one who had escaped the horror had been Ishtar's mother, who had been at home, and Raphael's two brothers. One was abroad training to be a doctor and the other was a policeman sent off to a remote posting.

In the weeks and months that followed shock waves swept over the city. No one had seen the coup coming and the country was now engulfed in fear and confusion. To begin with, some of the young people in the city would get together in the largest plaza where a waterless fountain stood. Gathering around Neptune and two open-mouthed stone fish, in a show of defiance, they appeared to flirt and talk and laugh out loud as if nothing had happened. They brought portable record players and played music to dance the tango. They did what young people did. But in reality they were touching on the subject of democracy. However, these gatherings did not last long. Very soon two boys were shot in full view of the town. After that the plaza emptied while the waterless fountain remained in the burning sun with only a few stray dogs for company.

That was when Raphael began to talk of the future. He could think of nothing else.

'Let's make a baby,' he said.

'Are you crazy?' Ishtar cried. 'Have you lost all your senses? Is this what grief has done to you?'

Raphael shook his head. There had been no funerals because, when they went to look for the bodies of those who had been machine-gunned down, none were to be found. Long lines formed every day outside every police station in every city and shanty town but no information was forthcoming. It seemed everyone knew of someone who had been on the street that morning. They were all in shock. Without a body, without a funeral, grief took on another dimension.

'Yes, *now*,' Raphael insisted. 'This is exactly the right moment.'

Ishtar stared at him. She was terrified. Had her husband lost his mind? She held her head in her hands and wept while Raphael stroked her dark hair. Didn't she *want* a child?

'What for?' she had shouted. 'To give it what kind of future?'

There were rumours that people were collaborating with the new regime. Who was collaborating with whom? Overnight they were witnessing the destruction of their country.

'Can't you see?' Ishtar cried. 'Who do we trust from now on?'

Until recently new recruits to the secret police had numbered amongst their friends. But Raphael didn't care. He had heard all the arguments for not having a baby. They had been his own arguments once but now, when *she* voiced them, he found them unbelievably depressing.

Ishtar was coping but only just. Raphael's craziness was wearing her down.

'All right,' she said finally. 'If this is what it has come to, all right.'

It was madness, of course. Ishtar missed her father but her mother was too frightened to come to live with them. She was scared of tainting Ishtar and Raphael with the same false suspicion that had tainted her husband.

Six more months passed and, although her mother begged them to stay away from her house, Raphael and Ishtar were determined to visit her no matter what. They decided to take the trip during the time of a public festival when other things distracted the troops. Cautiously they boarded a bus to the town where the widow lived. They walked quickly through the narrow streets until they reached her house. The street that had once been so lively was now silent in spite of it being a public holiday. Ishtar burst into tears when she saw her mother. Raphael looked around the bare home. All the widow's worldly possessions could have fitted into a trunk. Ishtar must have thought something like this too because it was then that she told her mother she was pregnant.

But now, having got what he had been pestering for, Raphael took on the despairing look of a man confronted by his vanished life. Why on earth had he wanted a child? He didn't dare tell Ishtar about these new feelings of doubt, not now she had given him such a gift. Eventually she prised his thoughts out of him. A row followed. Ishtar had always had a bigger temper than Raphael.

'Shut up!' she screamed. 'We have made a life. You got what you wanted, now be quiet. We will simply have to work with this ghastly situation.'

She placed her hand on her stomach. Then she took one of Raphael's hands and placed it there too, so he could feel the baby move. Neither of them spoke. In the half-light they observed each other crying silently. Lying awake long after

Ishtar had fallen asleep, Raphael worried about what they had done.

He was not a man who had ever taken an interest in politics but now he was being forced to do so. He decided to buy the book that the dictator had written and read it at work when he was alone. He felt he needed to understand this man who had taken the lives of their parents. What he found in that book was chilling. It seemed to be all about command and obedience. Was this the world Raphael was bringing new life into? Someone at the little observatory saw what he was reading and raised an eyebrow.

'Are you planning to leave astronomy and join the militia?' the man, a colleague called José, asked in a neutral voice.

Raphael understood José did not want to show his true feelings. Ashamed, he shook his head. He had worked with José for years; they had gone to university together, conducted their research together. And now he was afraid that Raphael was siding with the dictator by reading his book. Was this what life had come to?

'No, of course not,' he said.

José placed a finger to his lips. There was no knowing who might be listening. He came nearer to Raphael and looked through his telescope.

'All military men,' he whispered, 'want to become generals. And for this reason they will never contradict their superiors.'

Then, on a cloudless night of magenta and white stars, their daughter Helen was born and Raphael's entire life took on a new meaning.

Helen arrived at the last moment of twilight as darkness descended on the land. Raphael had been called from work and he travelled to the city hospital where Ishtar, united with her mother for this brief moment, lay in the bed waiting for him. It seemed to his dazzled eyes that the stars had never shone more brightly in the sky. Millions of sparks of light moved softly in the Milky Way, connecting to life on earth.

He had never seen anyone more beautiful than Ishtar that night as she lay holding his child and, when she gave him Helen to hold for the first time on his chest, he felt complete. Even the sadness of his parents' absence could not destroy that feeling. The simplicity of what Ishtar and he had done together gave him a happiness that he felt others spent their lives chasing.

'No matter what,' he told Ishtar, forgetting all his past anxieties, 'no one will ever take this moment from us!'

Afterwards, at the celebration party for Helen, a photograph was taken. The photo showed Raphael smiling happily as he held Helen with only one hand. Ishtar had one arm raised anxiously in case he dropped the child. But Helen was so tiny it was easy for Raphael to hold her in his one large hand. They were all smiling, even Ishtar's mother.

The photograph in its large important cardboard mount, with the name of the photographer's studio in gold letters, with its thin gold line that cost an extra sum of money, was with Raphael still. It had travelled across the world with him in the same way that once, long ago, he had wished to travel with his precious family. It was part of the vestiges from that other life. But although he looked at it most days, counting the dead within its frame, he could no longer see them as clearly as he once had.

IV

Helen was their greatest joy. Even the dictator and the new order he was creating could not dampen their delight in their child. Holding the baby in his arms, gazing at her sleeping face, Raphael was shocked by how much he loved her. He carried Helen with him everywhere. He travelled on the bus with the sleeping child against his heart. When she could not sleep at night, in spite of Ishtar's feeble protests, he took her outside and showed her the stars. He whispered in her ear that time passes but space does not. He told her not to be afraid of darkness because darkness was older than time.

'We don't know where darkness comes from,' he told the infant who moved her eyes like small telescopes across the sky, 'but without it as a curtain we would not see the stars.'

Hearing this nonsense one night, Ishtar laughed.

'You are such a fool, Rapho,' she said. 'Honestly!'

It had been a while since he'd heard Ishtar laugh and he was glad that something of his wife's sorrow was being healed by the presence of their daughter. Searching the night sky, he felt taken out of time entirely and the following day, when he had no work, he took Helen to the museum to look at religious paintings from the sixteenth century.

'These paintings, too,' he told the child, 'live outside time.'

He was still young enough to have hope. With Helen beside them, any mountain could be climbed.

'Look, Helen,' he would say, 'see what a beautiful mother you have! One day you, too, will look exactly like her!'

The months passed in this way. There were things that still annoyed them of course. The dictator's framed photograph appearing in every building incensed them both. The man was everywhere, in hospitals and banks and railway stations and by bus stops. Yet no one dared speak against him. And in the major cities, in cool gardens and palaces, beside fountains and under the shade of palm trees, the tango could still be heard. Dancing was still possible if you were in the dictator's inner circle. One evening, after work, Raphael brought home a map. He tacked it to the wall of their small living room. That evening, when the child was asleep, he and Ishtar stood looking at the world. It was Helen's world now and Ishtar felt they should make an effort to make it a better, safer place for her.

'We must be strong,' Ishtar said. 'We must fight this man.'

Raphael put his arm around his wife's slight shoulders. Always when she used this tone of voice it sent a small ripple of unease through him. She had made other comments like this in the same reckless way. As if Helen's birth had energised her.

'Stop talking like this,' he said lightly. 'You are a mother now. That is the most important job in the world. You can't be a revolutionary too!'

Ishtar was silent, frowning. 'You know why they killed my father, don't you?' she said.

Ishtar's father had known certain things.

'What sort of things?' Raphael asked.

'He suspected a coup of some sort was about to take place and he warned a politician friend of his.'

It was Raphael's turn to be silent. Then he changed the subject.

'Let's go to the sea again,' he said, giving his wife a loving, hungry look. 'Remember how happy we were there? Besides, we need to show Helen the ocean. It's part of her world.'

'Helen won't have much of a world if we don't stand up to the arsehole who has taken control of our country,' Ishtar said.

'Ishtar …' Raphael began.

Then he sighed. He loved his wife and didn't want to quarrel.

'Look, let's just show her the sea, shall we? Let's start with something small. Later we can change the world.'

Ishtar looked as if she might argue but the baby began to cry and her milk started to flow and distract her.

The three of them went down to the sea again. It was the last family holiday they would have together and everything about it was perfect. They went back to the little boarding house where they had stayed and the landlady, remembering them, had put a cot in the bedroom. When they first took Helen to the water's edge, she had cried and clutched Raphael with both of her tiny hands. Ishtar went plunging off into the waves and was soon swimming away from him so that it was he, Raphael, who dipped the child's feet in the foam, making her laugh. Later, when they had eaten a meal of fresh fish and Ishtar had fed Helen, they slept, all together in the wide soft bed. There was no need for a cot.

But Ishtar had changed. Her daughter's presence, rather than making her content, had made her restless. The trip to the sea had had only a limited effect on her mood. Instead of making her more cautious, the child was bringing out daring tendencies in her. She was angry about her father's death and that anger was beginning to stir. Why were they unable to talk about the terrible incidents that were taking place all over the country? Why be frightened even in the privacy of their own home? It was a ridiculous state of affairs. What had happened was an injustice. The world needed to know about it. Didn't it?

'Leave it, *querida*,' Raphael told her. 'Whatever you do won't bring our parents back.'

It was a comment guaranteed to send Ishtar into a frenzy of rage.

'Raphael!' she shouted. 'I remember the days when it was you and not I who was the rebel. What has happened to you, you coward?'

Raphael saw with a sudden sharp awareness that Ishtar and he no longer saw eye to eye on every subject.

The following evening he returned home to find Ishtar in another bad mood. She served their meal in silence and busied herself getting Helen to sleep. Unusually for her, she sang no lullaby.

'What's wrong?' Raphael asked when the child was finally asleep and the two of them were alone.

He wondered if he had done something bad. Ishtar didn't answer.

'What's the matter with you?' he asked, trying to put his arm around her. 'If you don't tell me, *querida*, how can I fix it?'

'You can't fix it,' Ishtar said in a subdued voice.

He waited. He knew she wouldn't stay silent for long. After a while she got up and lit a candle. Then she got two glasses and poured them both a drink. And then she switched off the light.

'This afternoon,' she said in a low voice, 'a group of teenagers went over to the old factory after school. I think there were about eight of them.' They had chosen a time just before the factory workers left work. 'The boys started painting "Say No to the Dictator!" all over the wall of the factory. They had got some red paint and a few big brushes.'

Raphael shook his head in disbelief. 'What the hell did they think they were doing?'

Ishtar held her hand up.

'Wait!'

The siren sounded and the workers had started pouring out through the gate.

'At first no one took any notice of the boys. Then one or two of the men must have noticed because they started laughing.'

Soon a few started clapping and whistling.

'Suddenly the militia arrived from nowhere. Someone must have tipped them off.'

The militia had megaphones and they used them to clear the street.

'One boy shouted out to the workers to resist the new government, to cause riots. The militia grabbed hold of him and started beating him. So his brother, who had just arrived, ran home to tell their mother …'

'Oh my God!' Raphael said under his breath.

'Wait! One of the militiamen followed him. He went to the house and grabbed the brother.'

The boy's mother started screaming.

'They forced the woman to give them one of her stockings and they tied the boy's hands behind his back with it. Then they commanded the mother to play some tango music on the record player while they took her youngest son out and shot him, first in both eyes and then in the head.'

The woman pleaded with the army to spare him until the last moment. The boy was only twelve. He hadn't been the one to paint the wall.

'D'you know what the man said?' Ishtar asked.

Raphael shook his head.

'*Other mothers have already cried. Now it's your turn!*'

Ishtar was shaking.

'Then they went out and shot his older brother,' Ishtar said.

Raphael finished his drink. Then he went into the small pantry and fetched the rest of the bottle.

V

When Helen was four Ishtar told Raphael she wanted to go back to work.

'What kind of work can you do now?' he asked, surprised, for before they had married Ishtar had been a journalist. Obviously she could not carry on with that profession unless she wanted to work for the government.

Ishtar gave a short laugh. 'Oh *yes*!' she said. 'I'm going to work for that man, right?'

'But there isn't a single newspaper you can write for any more,' Raphael protested.

'Well, you will be surprised,' Ishtar announced, calmly. 'I'm going to work for two people who have started one up. They've given me the job of subeditor to start with.'

'Who?' Raphael asked.

'I'm not allowed to say.'

'Don't joke,' Raphael said.

'I'm not. It's for your own safety, idiot. The fewer people who know the better.'

'Oh really,' Raphael said, sarcastically. 'And your safety? What about *that*?'

He was furious.

'I'll be fine,' Ishtar said. 'All I'm doing is a little subediting.'

The unease Raphael had been feeling in the years since their parents had been killed increased. He was hurt too. Why hadn't Ishtar told him about this idea before?

'Because you would have objected,' she said. 'You know you would have.'

El Rapidito went into underground circulation a few months later. Thankfully, Ishtar had nothing to do with that process. All she did was correct the spelling of the articles written by others. At least that was what she told Raphael. Most of the work, including the printing of the paper, took place in the back room of a haberdashery. Raphael had no idea who the editor or the other journalists were. He presumed they were old friends from Ishtar's journalism school days. He assumed they could be trusted.

But he continued to be nervous about the whole venture and now he and Ishtar had begun to argue. In their community there were many people who had been in favour of the coup. They would hang flags on the dictator's birthday. Raphael kept away from these people but Ishtar would walk amongst them fearlessly, pretending to agree with their views and entertaining the mothers of the children who were Helen's age. Then, when she'd finished showing her face around, she would go back to her work on *El Rapidito*.

Things came to a head the following spring when Raphael's colleague José was detained one night. They arrested him on his way home from work. Later that night, his mother came to see Raphael and Ishtar. She arrived around midnight. No one knocked on a door at that hour unless it meant trouble. Raphael ushered José's mother in. She was distraught. She had seen two dead men on the roadside, still clutching their bags, and she was certain José had been killed too.

'You must help him, Ishtar,' the mother begged. 'He worked for you. You must not abandon him.'

'*What?*' Raphael said. 'He *what?*'

'Didn't you know?'

Raphael shook his head.

'Ishtar, what have you done?'

'I'm not the one doing things,' Ishtar snapped.

Raphael stared at his wife. He could not believe what he was hearing.

'They found maps and a bomb in a warehouse,' José's mother said. 'They said these belonged to him. But José doesn't go to any warehouses, just the haberdashery store to pick things up or deliver things.'

'He doesn't come to the haberdashery store,' Ishtar said. 'He delivers his dispatches to another contact in San Antonio.'

Raphael looked from one to the other, aghast. He had no idea of the extent to which Ishtar had been hiding things from him.

'You never asked,' Ishtar said. 'So I didn't tell you.'

In spite of her defiant words Raphael saw she was shaken. He put his head in his hands. José was *his* friend. Why hadn't *he* said anything to Raphael either?

'Oh, they are quite good at discovering bombs whenever they take someone,' Ishtar said contemptuously.

'How d'you know?' demanded Raphael. 'How the hell do you know? What else do you know?'

There was a small sound. Helen woke up and began to call out for some water. The light in the room was dim. No breeze stirred the curtain; in the distance there was the sound of gunfire followed by a siren.

'Doesn't *she* matter to you, then?' Raphael asked in a savage whisper, pointing in the direction of the child.

José's mother was crying quietly. Raphael stood up. He glared at his wife. They had never really fought that much until now. They had always been on the same side but, now, he was less sure. Without a word he left the room and Ishtar heard him murmuring to the child.

After this incident Raphael began to consciously distance himself from Ishtar's work. He was frantic and hurt and the thought that anything might happen to Ishtar and therefore to Helen made him lie awake at night, worrying. But he never said a word to her. José was never seen again. At some point, maybe two years later, he went from being 'detained' to becoming one of the 'disappeared', leaving behind a family to feed for ever on only a slender hope.

VI

No one realised that the dictator could be this powerful. When the first wave of killings was over, the massacre of old and young alike, there had been a curfew followed by an eerie silence. Shock immobilised the country and then the disappearances started. José was one of the first to go. Any decent existence had become impossible.

You could have been walking on the street,
shopping,
running to catch one of the few buses that still operated,
arrive late for work,
have grey hair,
or glasses.
You might sneeze in a public place,
laugh too loudly – although God knows there was nothing to laugh about.
You might have forgotten your IDs. Or worse, offer an explanation as to why you'd forgotten it.
You might breathe at the wrong time and too loudly.
And then you would disappear.
For the regime, disappearance was better than dying because that way you numbered amongst the unaccounted-for.

The more disappearances occurred, the more determined Ishtar became. She was back writing her journalistic pieces under another name in spite of all Raphael's pleadings. Sometimes, when she returned towards dawn by some secret route, she would sleep in the spare room so as not to disturb Raphael. He worked in the observatory intermittently at nights in order to accommodate Ishtar's work. He was becoming more and more unhappy and often his thoughts turned towards the possibility of their leaving the country altogether – but he knew any hint of such an idea would merely enrage Ishtar. There was no way she would leave her home. Then the disappearances appeared to stop. Weeks passed and nothing happened. Cautiously, the cowering town began to relax. Perhaps life would return to normal. The dictator was seen on State television laughing and kissing babies, welcoming dignitaries from other countries, smiling and waving at the crowds on national holidays. The town of Santiopolis could not be blamed for thinking it was safe. No one wanted to come to this arid place where only stars thrived.

But Ishtar knew exactly what was going on. It was true Santiopolis appeared to be safe for the moment but this was a false peace and would not last. Ishtar knew that the disappearances were still taking place in other towns and in the capital city. In fact, if anything, they were happening more frequently. The only difference was no one talked any more and, because of the State control of the media, word did not always spread across the country. There were whole families who would simply vanish overnight. Relatives going to the police station would be asked to wait in a room from which they would never come out. The silence that surrounded these disappearances was impenetrable. Only the underground newspaper *El Rapidito* continued, through its network of contacts, to report the names of the disappeared. By now Ishtar was its editor-in-chief. No one knew where its head office was or who supplied the information to its editor, whose name was not disclosed. Circulation was surreptitious but the newspaper remained in existence.

And then what Raphael had dreaded happened.

The evening they came for Ishtar was dry and bright. The Milky Way rose up in all its majesty. It was an evening when Raphael was not at home. He had gone to work to record a meteorite shower. Ishtar's mother was with Helen while Ishtar was elsewhere, putting the latest edition of the paper to bed. From Ishtar to the journalists who filed copy, the people who came forward with the information, the printers and the distributors, all knew the risks. Yet all of them carried on with the work. Once a month some copies were even smuggled out to America where they were reproduced and distributed by hand. Raphael, who still hated what Ishtar did, had reluctantly admitted the necessity of the paper. Every evening on his way home he would look for a shooting star to wish his wife a safe return in the morning. He would remember for ever how, on the night they came for Ishtar, a whole shower of stars appeared again and again in the sky. Afterwards, he wondered if that had been Ishtar's way of saying goodbye.

They came to the house in the early evening, before dusk had set in, while the mountains were slowly turning a deep purple and the sky was still pink and soft. Ishtar's mother was sitting with Helen while she ate her evening meal. It was a woman who spoke to Ishtar's mother first. She sat at the kitchen table and talked in a friendly manner. She wanted

174

to know Ishtar's whereabouts. When the old lady refused to answer, saying she did not know, the woman smiled. The gap between the woman's teeth was so large that the smile came out as a leer. Then, with no warning, two men and another woman were in the room and Helen was lifted off her feet and taken out, screaming. She was bundled into a car. Ishtar's mother could still hear the screams of her granddaughter as the car revved its engine and sped away. Two men now restrained her. They were not violent; in fact, she was taken aback by their gentleness.

'Tell us where your daughter is and we will bring the child back,' one of them said.

It was a simple matter of an exchange, the other man said. A life for a life. Ishtar's mother understood. Who should she save? The old lady was crying.

'What will you do to my daughter?'

'We just want to ask her a few questions,' the officer in the military said. 'That's all.'

Ishtar's mother was told she had only a few more minutes before her granddaughter would be killed. But how did she know they would keep their word that her granddaughter would be returned?

'Trust,' the military man told her. 'You need to trust us.'

They were men of their word, they said.

Ishtar's mother had a choice and she made it. After that, for what remained of her life, she could always hear her only daughter's screams as she was tortured, and again at the moment of her death. After that, Ishtar's mother lost any voice of her own.

VII

No amount of enquiry would reveal what had happened to Ishtar, and Raphael needed to find a way to anaesthetise his pain in order to survive. In the early days, the weeks and months following her disappearance, sometimes, when Helen slept, he played a CD of old mellow tango music to calm himself. But the music simply gave him back tragedy. He saw that, without information, the imagination mutates and becomes deformed. With no final goodbye, no word or look exchanged between them he was slowly unravelling. He understood that in order to survive he would have to forget. But how? It was only when he studied the light transmitted from the past that he coped with the terrible pain of loss. He knew the present did not exist in the stars. The illusion that he had control of his own life had faded and the feeling that something beyond him had taken place grew more terrifying with each day. He had always known that a snake bite received as a child could kill you at the age of sixty. From this he knew that he would never get over what had happened. But he still had a daughter to care for. So he kept his grief to himself and carried on with his daily life. He no longer saw the bird of prey on his way back from work. Perhaps it, too, hated the dictator and had left the area. Then one day on the way to work he found a small shard of whitened bone. Picking it up, he ran his hand along its surface. He felt he had stumbled on the fault line that lay between brutality and civilisation.

That night he saw Ishtar in his dream and told her about the bone.

'Is it yours?' he asked.

'No,' the dream-Ishtar said, 'it is probably the work of your glorious killer bird.'

He had to admit the possibility of the bird being the culprit. He was both glad the bird was back and sad it had killed again.

'I know that bird is more important to you than the state of our country!' dream-Ishtar said.

And she laughed the joyous laugh she used to have as a young girl.

'It must have flown back from where it belongs,' she added, amused. 'That bird should not have come here. It must have had a faulty compass.'

'Tell me,' he whispered. 'Tell me more.'

And after a time he heard her answer.

'I *do* have something to tell you. When my mother makes *porotos con riendas* for Helen, remind her she must at least use good oil.'

He always woke depressed from these encounters. His capacity to dream was a terrible thing. He felt aftershocks constantly. How long ago did she say that? He doubted he'd ever understand the mystery of the human voice. How it stayed around haunting the corridors of memory long after the instrument that produced it had vanished. He thought about his capacity to go on loving Ishtar without the presence of her body. And each time he thought of her it felt like an act of creation because each time he thought of her differently.

By now Ishtar had been missing for seven months. Raphael had expected things to get easier but they had got a lot worse and he became frightened of the constant dreams. He knew a man could stop sleeping at night simply because of a fear of dreaming and some nights he didn't close his eyes. His daughter Helen continued to cry in her sleep. She still asked about her mother. On certain evenings, when it was too hot to do anything else, Raphael took her to the place beyond the old part of the city where grieving relatives often went if there had been no body to bury. It was a dusty, useless place and like everywhere in this desert city was encrusted with the debris left over from the bombings of many months. They did not go there too often. Helen was reluctant and Raphael did not like to keep talking about the disappearances to this small, delicate child.

During the day Ishtar's mother looked after Helen while Raphael was at work. The three of them were living a twilight existence. After another six months, Raphael became convinced Helen was slowly forgetting her mother and he tried to forget her too. Lately he had started going back to working at night. When he was absorbed in the stars, he could for a brief while forget his wife's disappearance, his daughter's unhappiness and the twenty thousand who had been killed. He knew his behaviour was laughable, yet he continued to believe that if he withdrew from his grief a little, it would give Helen some time to forget. Helen appeared to survive his moods and the daily problems of their life in the dust bowl and, for a time, things seemed marginally better, if better was a word that could be used for such a situation. And as always when he stared out at the dark sky he was certain he could suppress a lifetime's memories, put the earthly world behind him and focus on the universe. In this way, for a little while, he felt at peace.

One night, in the early spring of the following year, when Ishtar had been disappeared for over a year, he got a telephone call from a neighbour. His mother-in-law wanted him to come home quickly. His daughter had been taken ill. He hurried back and saw instantly that things were serious and Helen badly needed to be seen by a doctor. The old doctor who had been the family physician no longer lived in the town. Raphael did not know how to find him and none of the younger doctors who worked for the government were willing to come out at this time of night. There was nothing else for it and in desperation he contacted his brother Ares.

Ares had trained as a doctor in North America. After the coup he returned to the city with his American wife and his three children. He took up residence in a lush, green part of the city and became a prominent physician. He had had no contact with the rest of his family after their parents died and even when Ishtar was taken from Raphael, Ares did not come to visit his brother. Raphael hadn't cared much. He understood that Ares was an ambitious man who wanted to stay on the right side of the regime. And if that meant forgetting about his relatives so be it. But now things had changed. Pride did not come into it. Helen needed help. Even if he would not see his niece, Ares would know someone who could. Raphael called him. Ares grumbled at the inconvenience.

'I can't come out in the curfew, you know I can't. And nor should you; you might get shot. Then what would your daughter do?'

Ares lived eight kilometres away; there were no buses at

this time of night. It was dangerous to go walking after dark. Ares complained that it was also dangerous for him to receive visitors at this hour. What if Raphael got him into trouble with the authorities? But Raphael told him stubbornly that he was coming and he then hung up.

'I'll be as quick as I can,' he told his mother-in-law, placing his hand on his child's hot forehead.

Helen had drifted off into an uneasy sleep after hours of screaming.

It was a Friday night and the soldiers were out on patrol. It took Raphael an hour to walk to his brother's house but he managed to avoid the main road with its army checkpoints. By the time he arrived, apart from one light at the back, the house was in darkness. A strong scent of jasmine and tuberose filled the air, bringing Ishtar's funeral wreaths sharply to mind. Raphael threw some gravel through the open shutters and instantly the light was switched off. He heard his brother coming down the outside stairs in his slippers. They greeted each other with a nod. Ares did not invite Raphael inside the house nor did he offer him a drink of any kind. They sat instead on a bench in the cool garden amongst the lush vegetation. Even the heat seemed less intense. A slight breeze sprang up, lifting the leaves of the paw-paw plant.

'I wish I could help you,' Ares said at last when Raphael finished speaking. 'But you know it is impossible for me to prescribe medicine without seeing the patient first. I might get struck off.'

Ares sat smoking. Raphael was too proud to ask for a glass of water.

'Please,' he said, instead, 'no one would know.'

Ares shook his head. 'I'm sorry.'

Raphael stared at his brother in disbelief.

'She is your niece!' he said appalled. 'Tomorrow might be too late.'

Ares was silent. He put two fingers in his mouth and took out a scrap of food, then flicked it away. Then he threw the butt of his cigar into the bushes. Turning away towards the house, he looked up at the windows.

'You know what, brother, I have a wife and children. I have another child on the way.'

He reminded Raphael of a conversation they had had long ago when the Terror was rumoured to be on its way. What will you do when the time comes to stand up and be counted? What *should* you do?

'When you get to my age,' Ares said in a sharp whisper, 'you will understand, Raphael.'

There was the sound of an army truck somewhere in the distance and then coarse laughter. Ares walked back to the house and, as Raphael watched, he raised a hand in farewell. Then he went inside and softly closed the huge green doors. It was, Raphael thought, as if they were not related.

Helen died in a windowless room of complications resulting from meningitis. She was just six years old.

VIII

When Helen died Raphael went properly crazy. He no longer cared about anything at all. Someone, a man he vaguely knew, approached him soon after the funeral and recruited him to the cause. The man was pretty shrewd. He knew Raphael had nothing more to lose, so he offered him an outlet for all those things boiling inside him. Because he worked at night it was easier to move around without being noticed. His boss, having had a rare moment of empathy that transcended the political situation, suggested Raphael took a break. He agreed and straight away became a gun-runner for the freedom fighters. He went all over the place under cover of darkness. These trips to the jungle took him away from his city and from the unmarked graves of the men and women he once had known, talked to and even shared a drink with. It took him away from the smaller graves of the children who had died since the coup. Because of this he began to love the jungle. He decided to leave his job altogether, take on casual work and use his grief as an excuse to avoid suspicion. It was a darker kind of place that he was entering now but, really, he didn't care. He kept telling himself he had nothing to lose. Or so he thought.

Then one day his car was stolen. His car had never been

stolen before. It was a queer sort of time for it to go missing, too. Midday. Who would steal a car in broad daylight? He went to the police to report it and a man, a teenager really, took the details. Then another officer came out to talk to him. Later Raphael went to see his youngest brother, Achilles. Raphael got on well with this brother although they didn't see much of each other. Achilles was a nickname given to him after an accident to his heel when he was still a boy. Achi worked strange hours and was often transferred to other parts of the country at short notice. He was a policeman, not a corrupt cop but someone who did his job without fuss while secretly opposing the regime. When they met they embraced each other warmly. The last time Raphael had seen this brother had been at Helen's funeral. He had not been very conscious at the time but Achi had embraced him and comforted him as best he could. Achi had divorced his wife recently. He lived alone and drank heavily.

'What's going on?' Raphael asked, looking around the apartment. He was shocked by the state of the place.

Raphael noticed that all the furniture was in the centre of the room and covered in dust.

'Oh, the bombs,' Achi said. 'I'm sick of cleaning up the glass so I moved everything.'

Two strips of electrical tape seemed to be holding the window closed.

'I think someone's following me,' Raphael said.

'Of course. Why are you surprised?'

Achi knew what his brother was involved in. They had not discussed it but each assumed that they knew the same people, only from different sides.

'What's happened? Why are you on foot?'

'My car was stolen. In broad daylight.'

'So that in itself doesn't mean anything.'

Raphael shook his head. 'No, listen. I reported it to the police. The policeman wrote everything I said down. He looked up the registration number; he looked at my ID. Then an officer came out and told me they had found my car.'

Stolen cars did not reappear so suddenly. They both knew that.

'They took me to it, right where I had left it. Nothing was damaged; it was exactly as I had left it.' Raphael paused and leaned over towards Achi. 'Everything was there, except for my briefcase.'

'You sure?'

'Yep.'

'Did you tell them?'

Raphael nodded.

'You shouldn't have,' Achi said. 'What did they say?'

'"So you are some sort of messenger, huh?"'

'And you said?'

Raphael paused, taking a deep breath. He hadn't slept. 'I said, "Where's my fucking briefcase?"'

'Raphael,' Achi said.

He stood up abruptly.

'I know what has happened to you makes you no longer care. I know it has all been terrible ...' He hesitated. 'I was going to come over when I finished my shift this weekend to see you. What's all this about you quitting your job?'

'Who told you?'

Achi sighed. 'Raphael, why do you trust people?'

He moved towards the kitchen and turned the tap on. Then he pointed at the ceiling and beckoned Raphael to come nearer to the tap. The room was bugged. Achi took out a piece of paper and wrote on it. Then he handed it to Raphael. Raphael stared at the paper.

Some of those fighters are double agents, it said.

Why do you tell people things?

You are endangering others as well as yourself. Me for one.

I know you don't care about your life.

Being killed is one thing. Being tortured is another.

You should leave this place.

Raphael took the pencil from his brother and wrote:

I cannot leave Ishtar and Helen behind.

Don't be an idiot, Achi wrote. *Ishtar and Helen are dead. They can travel with you wherever you go.*

Raphael swallowed. He thought of the graves, marked and unmarked. Overhead in the endlessly blue sky the planes were swooping low. Elsewhere, some village was about to be destroyed. Dust would cover the blood that dried in the heat. Women would at this very moment be raising their arms in that now famous gesture of grief. In Achi's kitchen the tap continued to run. Achi switched on the ceiling fan and appeared to relax a little.

I want you to leave, he wrote.

I can get you out.

Raphael stared.

Where would I go?

Achi hesitated. Then he wrote:

LONDON.

He crumpled the piece of paper and glanced up at the ceiling. Raphael knew that he would burn the paper later.

It would take nearly a year for this suggestion to take root and, in that time, many things would happen to add more guilt to Raphael's already guilt-soaked mind. The first of these was the murder of a man whose name had been in the notebook in his briefcase. The death was particularly gruesome and went unnoticed in the town until someone smuggled a blurred photograph to the Western press. The image had been taken with only a cheap camera but its brutality was indisputable. It went around the world and then a week later everyone except Raphael forgot about it. He went over to see the man's widow and drank a glass of soda he did not want while watching her cry. He had gone to show his respects but really all he could feel was the hostility of the family in the hot, dusty room. It was his fault. This war was killing him too, he wanted to tell them.

'I'm sorry,' he mumbled.

And he left the house, their anger and their grief chasing him up the hill to the bus stop.

Five days later his car was torched. Three days after this incident, a wooden mechanical horse was wheeled into the city for the annual puppet show. With hundreds of moving parts and twenty-two pumping pistons, this remarkable horse was made of fifty-six square metres of hardwood. It had flapping leather ears and deep wrinkles around the eyes. The body had a small door built into it that housed a room where the puppeteer could ride. But its steel skeleton was hidden from view.

The town buzzed with amazement. For the people of the dusty forgotten town it was a small miracle that the government had chosen their town for this puppet festival. It helped them to forget the terrors of the last few years.

IX

Raphael wasn't interested in the puppet festival. The puppet festival was for children and he had no child to take with him. As usual he was tired and depressed; more depressed than usual. He had gone to bed early and for once had fallen into a dreamless sleep when something, some noise, awakened him. He thought it was the call of a bird of prey. Sitting up in bed, he stared into the darkness before reaching for his trousers. His feet were on the floor; he was about to stand up when an arm wound around his neck from behind. A hood was tugged roughly over his head and his arms pulled back sharply. He heard before he felt the crack of a bone and then he screamed. And passed out. When he came round he was sitting in a pool of urine and shit. Someone was groaning and it was a moment longer before he realised the noise was coming from him. It was pitch dark and the pain in his bound arm was terrible. He gagged, partly because of this and partly because of the stench. A moment later he was being waterboarded.

Some time must have passed, how long he could not say, but he was still alive when they shone the light on his face and slapped him hard with the rubber tubing. He was still blindfolded. And naked. For ever after he would associate nakedness with death. When the interrogation started he couldn't understand what he was being asked. Comprehension was beyond him. They slapped him again and then gave him an electric shock on the soles of his feet. He screamed. And passed out once more. This business went on for days. Loudspeakers sent out instructions to stop him sleeping and microphones listened to his every groan night and day. He could hear nothing but the pounding of his own blood. They kept asking for a confession but what was he meant to confess? He cried out in despair. He had not killed anyone, he told them, but this, too, seemed to anger them and so they gang-raped him, laughing. He gathered *they* were the army.

'Now you will eat your own shit,' they promised, still laughing.

And they pushed shit into his mouth. He wanted death but it would not come. He prayed for it as though it was his God but still it did not appear.

The men did other things to him that he did not want to think about afterwards. Their depravity was of an astonishingly creative nature and, in a dim half-conscious way, in fleeting moments between the horror of it, he detached himself sufficiently to marvel at their talent for cruelty. There were ordinary household objects that they now used on him in extraordinary ways, handling them as casually as they might have in normal life. They came towards him as though they were doctors about to cure him, with the same calm behaviour as a medic might have.

Pain became his constant companion for months on end. Actually he had no idea how long he was in that place. When they finally threw him out, knowing he wasn't any use to them, he was almost blind in one eye because of the ballpoint pen they had jabbed into it. The brilliance of the sunlight outside astonished him. He slept in a dust-covered ditch for days, his only companions being the stray dogs, as thin as he was, that roamed the area. His wounds became septic before he was able to crawl for help. Luckily for him the old doctor his family had known found him. The doctor had been banned from practising medicine after the coup, which was why Raphael hadn't been able to find him when Helen had been ill. When he stumbled across Raphael he was horrified. He barely recognised the man he had once known as a boy. He was shocked to hear about the child's death and Ishtar's disappearance. Hiding his horror, the doctor put Raphael into the back of his truck. Then, not caring whether anyone had seen him or not, he drove him to his house.

'You are luckier than most people,' the doctor told him. 'Most people do not survive that place.'

Raphael did not answer. He did not weep either. All his tears had dried up some time ago, but when he did eventually speak it was with such bitterness that the doctor could only bow his head in acknowledgement. Luck was not the correct word, he said.

The doctor hid Raphael in an underground bunker at the bottom of his garden and put him back together slowly, as though he was a jigsaw. He warned Raphael that some things were not fixable. It was many more weeks before he found out that Achi had disappeared. The doctor made a few discreet enquiries but the leads all ended in culs-de-sac. That was that.

'Don't expect to hear from your brother,' he said, shaking his head. 'The police don't tolerate disloyalty, I know.'

Raphael didn't tell the doctor about Ares. There seemed no point.

Three months after he had been released, although his wounds were still infected, the doctor told Raphael that he had organised a visa for him.

'You must leave,' he said. 'Don't think they are finished with you.'

Raphael began to shiver. The temperature outside was over forty but he was cold.

'I'm sorry,' the doctor said. 'I've done what I can but if you don't go they will come back and kill you.'

'And you, too,' Raphael said at last, his voice coming out in a croak.

The old man shrugged. That wasn't the point, he told Raphael. They would kill him, too, anyway at some point but he was too old to care. All his family had gone. Raphael opened his mouth to say it was the same for him but the old man held up his hands in protest.

'You are young enough to take a message into the world. This is important. What this whole country has suffered is no small thing.'

It took a while to persuade Raphael.

'Where can I go?' he asked. 'Who will want someone like me?'

The old doctor was silent for a long time. He stared out at the great dusty expanse of sand and rubble that was as large as an ocean. The sun beat mercilessly down; the day was shadowless and full of an invisible and unspeakable grief. Nothing would completely erase it; nothing would heal this place for a hundred years.

'England,' the doctor said softly. 'I have a contact there. You will be safe. There will be doctors who will help you. And you must talk to them about those you have left behind.'

England, thought Raphael. He knew nothing of England. He tried to imagine what Ishtar might make of this but Ishtar seemed to have receded to some place beyond his reach. How could he leave her behind?

'I must find something of her,' he said in a waterfall of grief. 'Something I can take with me. Helen too.'

The doctor shook his head.

'You can't go out looking,' he said. 'First, you do not have the strength. The burns are third degree; you must stay in the shadows. But in any case they have placed barbed wire all over the desert. You won't even be able to get close.'

It was a second before Raphael realised what this would mean for him. He stared at the old man and saw that life was now hell-bent on moving him away from his material past. He felt a shudder go through his body. Ishtar! He had not dared to voice her name until now.

Ishtar.

His wife. The mother of Helen.

The disappeared.

Why did he need to search for her bones?

He could not explain the desire to know her resting place. He knew the rumour that the remains of the disappeared had been tipped into the sea. So why search the desert?

To disappear is to exist somewhere, he felt.

The doctor nodded in agreement. His eyes were bright. He had his own story too painful to tell.

To disappear is to live in the world.

Only the dead are truly dead.

Only they can become stars.

He wished, instead of the telescope that searched the sky, there might exist an instrument to search the ocean.

Ishtar.

Existing neither on land nor water.

'One day they will get tired of the barbed wire,' the doctor said. 'They will get tired of protecting the evidence; they will find other things to interest themselves. When that happens they will calm down, look away, wonder what all the anger was about. They will be a little embarrassed, shamefaced even. And because they won't want to be reminded of what they did together they will move away and leave the desert to us.'

In the silence that followed the doctor's words, Raphael heard a bird call repeatedly. It reminded him that beyond his limited horizon were other places, the sea even, still beautiful and unchanged from all those years ago when he had visited it. At least, he thought, there are still peaceful places in the world. 'When that day comes,' the doctor said, picking up the fragile thread of his own thoughts, 'I will find you a shard of bone from your past. And send it to you.'

X

Raphael Kalchas carried his memories across an ocean wracked by storms. Hours of grey turbulence could not muffle his pain. Loneliness smote him. Thoughts were useless and England, when it came to him, was not as he expected. He noticed things others did not. He noticed it was not cold in the way it could be in his own country. The cold here was simply a dampness that crept into his bones, not like the crisp cold of the mountain ranges of his country, where snow and sea lived together in harmony. Home called to him through his broken limbs and the dull ache of his destroyed body. When the doctors at the Foundation first examined him, their gentleness was such that he was first rendered speechless. Their kindness was a powerful thing. And at long last he wept. Now he saw how broken he really was and he wanted to die. And at this point the images of Ishtar and Helen began blurring, merging, confusing him.

'Don't worry,' the psychiatrist said. 'It can sometimes be this way. Later on it will separate out. Wait. Be patient with yourself.'

The psychiatrist was an African. Once, long ago, he too had been tortured. Even before he found this out, Raphael's instinct was to trust him and this small act was in itself healing. So he tried to believe the images of Ishtar and Helen would come back to him. That, like the stars, with time they would separate out from the thousands who had died with them. He was prepared to wait, he told the psychiatrist.

'Begin again,' the psychiatrist advised. 'You can visit the Underworld but you cannot live there for ever.'

After this advice Raphael cried for three days.

Long after he was discharged, he tried to follow this rule. The people at the Foundation helped him get a job. It wasn't the kind of work he had once had but it required little effort and, for a while, until his health worsened, he remained there. The people he worked with were from twilight zones also. Small things occurred that oiled his painful passage through this time. Someone, an anonymous Good Samaritan, left money for him, and others at the Foundation helped him too. He was silenced by this generosity but something had begun to close up in him now and he found it difficult, after that first flood of emotion, to articulate his feelings.

'Don't worry,' the psychiatrist said again. 'That too will change with time.'

It was the only thing the psychiatrist got wrong.

When he moved to his current house it took him seven years to build his telescope. There were many reasons for this. One was that the telescope was made of recycled objects and he had to wait for exactly the right thing to be found. He spent hardly any money. This was something he was good at because of the long years of the war. Sometimes, during those seven years, he would wake at night with his face wet with tears. Then, in those sleepless early still-dark hours, he would open up his maps of the galaxy and stare at them.

He would run his finger along the list of places on the

moon, as familiar to him as the names of the roads where he now lived.

The Sea of Nectar

The Craters:

> Archytas
>
> Aristoteles
>
> Heymans
>
> Aliacensis
>
> Arzachel
>
> Alphonsus
>
> Ptolemaeus

Like rosary beads, they gave him comfort.

He spoke to hardly anyone in these years. Everyone in his small patch thought he was very old.

Finally, the telescope was built but he needed help installing it. He had no friends in the neighbourhood. Most people in the street left him alone and, because of the cuts to social services, he was visited by a social worker only twice a year. In the end someone from the Foundation came over and helped him get it working. At last he could gaze at his beloved stars.

The telescope was Raphael's lifeline. All through those last days before he left the doctor's house he had thought of nothing but the desert. He wanted to walk in it, to examine the dust, the rubble, the stones. He wanted to find some small piece of Ishtar in the ground. The word on the street before his arrest had been confusing. According to the rumours, the disappeared had been killed and dumped in mass graves, possibly somewhere in the vast desert. But he had never been able to find this spot. In his head a conversation he'd once had with Ishtar played over and over again.

'Our origins are not in the ground,' he'd said, 'but in the stars.'

Now, looking through his slowly turning telescope, he began to understand how every night the centre of the galaxy passed over every city in the world. Every night then, he was being connected to Ishtar and to Helen. And to his brother Achi. And so, every night he looked up at the Milky Way in the hope he was connecting with those he loved via the stars. This transformed his life as far as it possibly could.

One morning he went back to the Foundation. He had been discharged a year before but he wanted to speak to the psychiatrist who had treated him in those first fragile days. He knew exactly what he wanted to tell him.

'In the beginning I used to cry more than I spoke,' he would say. 'But because of you, I now speak more than I cry.'

All the way on the bus into central London he rehearsed what he would say. He wanted to talk about his telescope too and his discovery about the stars. He wanted to tell the psychiatrist that memory had a gravitational pull that cannot be denied and that because of this he was connected with his loved ones.

But when he arrived at the reception desk at the Foundation he was told he could not see the psychiatrist. The man had died of a heart attack a week before. Raphael had missed him by only a few days.

When he had recovered a little from the shock, another doctor came to see him in the waiting room where he sat. This doctor was a woman and, although she looked very tired and was clearly overworked, she spent some time talking to Raphael.

'All it takes is a puff of air,' she told him sadly, 'to destroy the present. But this does not mean you should give up. Those things you love are in the past. Don't give up on the past.'

Going back to the place he now called home, he understood certain things. He understood that he was the last-remaining survivor of history. He, Raphael, was a transmitter of history and also of memory.

When he arrived at his front door he found the cat waiting for him. That was the first day of their uneasy association with each other. It was now that he decided to drop the name Dr Kalchas. From now on he called himself simply Raphael.

22.

UNCLASSIFIED/NOT FOR PUBLIC RELEASE

thinking of you all is like having good food so I think of each of you all the time.

nnnnnn asked me if I wanted some water. We were in the ▪▪▪▪ block of the ▪▪▪▪

centre I cried without tears. All the tears came early on during the flight to ▪▪▪▪. I thought of you Mum and you Hera and even you Dad. I thought of all the wrong things I did, how I was rude to you Dad. While I was having this daydream I was fine, almost happy. Did I used to be happy once? They are ▪▪▪ ▪▪▪▪▪▪ ▪▪ ▪▪ ▪▪▪▪ One of the ▪▪▪▪▪▪ looks so ▪▪ ▪▪▪▪ that I can't believe he is human. I don't know if this letter is going to get to you. I miss you all so much. One thing I realised is that a. I am going to grow old or die here and b. no one really can empathise with anyone. The trouble is that they can't get into my head and imagine what it must be like.

When you take away all of a person's clothes you humiliate them in a way that is not quite believable. I have to stand there and be interrogated for hours. They laugh at me, scream and spit. They bring their faces so close to mine I can see the fine blonde hairs on their chins. I can see the pores, the whiteheads. I can see they are out of control. The switch has been turned the other way and they are drunk with the pleasure of what they do to me.

When the ▇▇▇▇▇ begins it is usually at ▇▇▇▇▇ in ▇▇▇ ▇▇▇ I think they can get themselves up to a frenzy when it gets dark. Like ▇▇▇▇. Sometimes they take me to ▇▇ ▇▇ ▇▇ ▇▇ just before the sun sets and once they took me out and forgot to put the bag on my head. So I saw the sun set. The light was so wonderful, orange that slowly faded to rose. I suppose it sank into the ocean eventually but I could not see it. I thought I would hate the colour orange but after seeing that sunset I will not hate a simple colour. I am going to make my mind strong enough not to hate it. A colour can do no harm. A colour isn't to blame for what ▇▇ and ▇▇ and the ▇▇ ▇▇ do to me.

yesterday. After they finished with me I was almost dead. A piece of bleeding flesh. Then they hosed me down and ▇▇ said ▇▇▇ ▇ ▇▇ ▇▇. I tried to smile at him but I was bleeding from my mouth.
This is nothing sonny boy ▇▇ said. I could believe it.

how are you all managing? I can imagine mum you are crying a lot and that Hera is being the strong one. Don't smile Hera I know what you are like. You must remain strong. They told me yesterday that ▮▮▮▮ ▮▮▮▮ would ▮▮▮▮ but it didn't happen. I waited all day in dread and then towards night ▮▮▮▮ ▮▮ ▮▮ and ▮▮▮▮ came to take me out.

'So you like looking at the sun set, huh?' they said.

And they laughed. I began to shiver. What were they going to do now? But all of a sudden ▮▮▮▮▮▮ ▮▮▮▮▮▮ took my arm, the one that they ▮▮▮ and took me out into the yard.

'Look,' he said. 'There, over there is ▮▮▮▮▮▮.'

I was crying for you. How is this possible that I can change into this blubbering person in such a short time? Is the distance in time between civilised living and hell so narrow?

I must try to talk to the guard ▮▮▮ I have a slight feeling that he is human, that he feels sorry for me. We are the same age ▮▮

▮▮▮▮▮▮▮▮▮▮ was the worst of all. how can the ▮▮▮ ▮▮▮▮▮▮▮ allow such sadistic cruelty? What kind of mind is capable of doing this sort of thing?

I couldn't write because two of my fingers are broken. The ▇▇▇▇▇▇ says it will mend. He doesn't sound too bothered. You see empathy there, that word again.

I have been counting the days by scratching a mark on the floor each day. So far no one has noticed. Sometimes ▇▇▇ and ▇▇▇▇▇▇▇ like to play a trick on me.

'Hey ▇▇▇▇,' they say. 'what would your mom say if she could see you now with a diaper on!'

I don't think this letter will ever get to you, which is why I am writing these things down. Someone, a soldier called ▇▇▇▇▇▇ told me I would get a lawyer from ▇▇▇▇▇▇ but nothing has happened so far. I'm guessing we are quite far away. Either ▇▇▇▇ or ▇▇▇▇. But of course I might be all wrong and this might be The Arena

I would like to believe there is a God. Funny how when I started out I used to laugh at you Dad and your worry beads, and your prayers but here, now I'm turning into you! When they allow us the call to prayer I pray like a devotee. You would laugh if you saw me ... well probably not laugh! At nights sometimes when I am in ▇▇▇▇ ▇▇▇▇ I get to see the stars. They are amazing here. The air is very dry and clear and one of the ▇▇▇▇ ▇▇▇▇ told me the names of two of them. After that I got very excited and wanted to study the sky. I wanted to get free of my body and fly away. Who was it said you rather looked at the stars or at the ground. I definitely want to be someone who looks at the stars. Yesterday when I was again in ███ ███ ███ asked me how I could be so cheerful. He doesn't know that I can cry with my mind, without tears, without one single sound. Maybe this has to be my life forever.

Mum and Dad and Hera I love you.

23.

Under the slate-grey eye of the sky the snow seemed to increase. The thermometer showed that the temperature was falling more steeply.

Having fled my mother's grave, leaving those that wept, without pausing to think of either Hektor or Lyle, I went to you, Raphael. Like a homing bird. Instinctively I had known only you could comfort me. And comfort me you did in all the ways I had longed for. You staunched that terrible wound, listened to me speak, carried my pain. And then, finally, hesitantly, told me your own shocking story. So that at last I truly understood you. Yes, beyond the overload of grief I was shocked – but perhaps I didn't say enough.

'You are tired,' I said, afterwards.

'Why do you say that?' you asked.

'The way you kissed me is tired.'

You sighed, not disagreeing. Giving me your past had exhausted you.

'There aren't that many years between us, you know,' I said tentatively. 'Not in our minds, I mean.'

You were silent for so long I thought you had fallen asleep.

'The years don't matter,' you said, finally. 'It isn't the years that frighten me.'

Afterwards I watched you for a long time as you slept. Then at 5 a.m. I left. A sudden great restlessness had come over me. I needed to be alone. And so I left you, meaning to return. Dawn had not broken. My mother lay in her cold grave. Never again would I feel her calloused hands on my face, never again hear her voice. In the last weeks after Aslam was taken I had become Calypso's mother but now I needed some mothering myself. In that moment, Raphael, as I softly closed the door on your sleeping self, not even you could have helped me. A woman's mother is the strongest influence that exists on her life. No man can compete with it. There was no sign of Hektor or Lyle.

In the empty house all that remained to mark the previous day's events was a copy of the holy book. Going upstairs I stared at the old rooms, Aslam's, mine, my parents'. The buried and the disappeared surrounded me but the house was unmoved by anything. Calypso's burka was in a plastic bag. Someone, probably Iris, must have brought it back from the hospital. In the darkness of the burial ground, underneath the snow, my mother had looked like a young girl again. Lyle, broken by grief, could only watch the ceremony and it had been Hektor with his ready tears who had wept the most. Now I stared at the things on her dressing table: her orange lipstick, a hardened bottle of nail polish, no longer of use to her, a comb holding strands of her black hair, an empty bottle of lily-of-the-valley perfume. In a trance I opened a drawer and found one of Aslam's shirts, neatly ironed. Frowning, puzzled, I stared. Why was it so familiar? Then I realised. Calypso must have bought an identical shirt to the one Aslam had worn on the day they took him. Something inside me was breaking. In that ironed shirt with its brightly coloured parrots lay Calypso's unspoken love. I felt I had hardly known my mother until now. Only grief truly teaches you the extent of love. I stared at that shirt for a long time. Then I saw there were other things I had not seen before.

A photograph of Lyle taken in some remote place that I did not recognise.

My brother on a bicycle with a smile that now needed memory to flesh it out.

The scent of roses, lingering long after all the flowers had gone.

Swallowing two of Calypso's sleeping pills, I sank into an exhausted and hallucinatory sleep. The dead could not have slept more deeply. Then, when the light sent its fingers through the pink faux-satin curtains, I stirred and went back to sleep again. What was there to wake up for? When eventually I surfaced from that drugged sleep of despair, it was with the vague unease that something else had happened. It was a moment before I remembered.

Aslam

Calypso

Their names jumbled and jarred in my mind as I staggered to the window and stared out at the deserted street. I had no idea what time of day or even what day it was and still I did not think of my father or of Lyle. There was no sun. There would be no sun for several years. The room was cold and in disarray. I had been sleeping in my parents' room on Calypso's side of the bed. Just as I had done as a child, when I was ill, or upset. At any moment Calypso might have walked in with a cup of coriander tea. I felt I was going mad.

Calypso

Aslam

Their names swung around again, hitting me with force so that I held on to the windowsill to stop myself from falling. Then a knock on the door. Had I known, would I have pleaded for a minute longer?

Just one more minute, please, to let me sleep through what I am just about to wake to.

Police!

What now? What did they want of me now? They had taken my brother; killed my mother. What more did they want? I had slept with all my clothes on. So I drew my coat closer and went slowly to answer the door.

24.

Although I didn't know this at the time, Lyle would miss the accident by twelve hours. Unknown to any of us, he'd left for the airport almost immediately after Calypso's funeral. There had been some rumours that flights were becoming infrequent because of the fuel problem and he was petrified that he'd never get to the Arena. I would not hear from him for months and, when I did, he simply reiterated his promises to Calypso. No matter what, he would rescue Aslam. Because of this he missed Hektor's accident. And so the police came to me first.

It wasn't simply that Hektor had had an accident. No. Although at first that was all the police told me. All the usual stuff was said to start with.

'We're really sorry, miss. Your father is in intensive care following an accident in the Rowthorn tunnel, north of the river.'

'No, no, he's still alive, don't worry.'

'It's Hera, isn't it, love?' the policewoman asked.

How different she sounded now.

'Your brother...' Her voice trailed off; she looked embarrassed.

I had been holding a bottle of sleeping pills when they

came for me. All I wanted was some water and to go back to sleep. To be honest, I had to concentrate really hard to assimilate anything they were saying.

'You want me to come?' I asked.

They nodded. My head was swimming, speech wasn't easy, and they seemed to understand this because they were patient with me. The policewoman gently took the bottle of pills out of my hand and handed me my keys. There was a car waiting outside. I remember thinking how unusually kind they were being to me. Not at all as they had treated Calypso.

In the car with a police officer on either side of me, I mumbled, 'My brother doesn't know our mother has died. I need to tell him …'

My voice trailed off into a wobble.

'It's okay,' one of them said. 'He knows. We've sent the news over.'

I swallowed.

'Don't worry, love. He knows.'

Love, I thought, amazed even in my drugged-up state. Who were these people? My eyes filled up. And then, suddenly, like a shot in the arm, remembering you, Raphael, I became desperate. I wanted to get back to you as fast as possible. But clearly that was not an option.

The hospital they took me to was the same one in which Calypso had lain, waiting to be buried. Hektor lay somewhere in its depths but they didn't take me to him straight away. Instead I was ushered into a room where a man and a woman in plain clothes were sitting. There was a tape recorder on the table and two files. They stood up and came towards me. They were not smiling but they were not unfriendly either as they extended their hands, which I ignored. When I sat on

211

the chair they provided the policeman went out and closed the door behind him. I was alone with the doctors. Only they weren't doctors.

They showed me two things.

One: a one-way air ticket to a city near to where all the fighting was going on and where the ancient temple had been blown up. The ticket was in Aslam's name but had been found on Hektor's person when he'd had the accident.

'Could you shed any light on this?' the man from Counter Terrorism asked me.

I shook my head, which was fast clearing.

'It would be helpful if you could think hard, see if anything, any small piece of information, springs to mind. Your brother's eventual release might hinge on it.'

Were they blackmailing me or being genuinely helpful?

'Your mother …'

'My mother is dead,' I said. 'May I see my father?'

'Yes, of *course* you can,' the man said quickly. 'Just as soon as we finish this conversation.'

I began to get agitated.

'I don't know anything,' I said, trying not to cry. 'All I know is they came for Aslam. He hadn't done anything wrong and taking him away has destroyed my entire family.'

Counter Terrorism nodded. Had these people been born without emotion or had they been trained this way? Could they not see I knew absolutely nothing?

They showed me the second thing. It was a small book entitled *The Destruction of Memory*.

'So?' I asked.

'It's a book about the destruction of ancient statues and buildings. Now you might remember how the Desert Death

Squad destroyed the temple in Aegilips? And then again the amphitheatre on the banks of the Achelous?'

And now the questioning began in earnest.

'Have you seen this book before?'

'Do you know why your brother was reading it?'

'Do you know why he kept quoting it on his blog posts?'

'The message in this book is about cultural genocide. Do you understand what this means?'

'What was it doing in the car of a *taxi driver*?'

I stared at my interrogators. Which one of us was insane?

And now I had a few questions of my own. How did they know the book belonged to Aslam?

'Take a look,' Counter Terrorism said, pushing it towards me.

I opened it and saw Aslam's name.

'It's not his handwriting,' I said flatly.

Counter Terrorism smiled and they shook their heads.

'We would like you to talk to your father, Hera,' the man said, using my name for the first time. 'See if he can shed any light on the airline ticket. That at least might help your brother.'

I stood up. I didn't realise I was crying. In that moment and with a kind of sick horror I understood what I never had before: that the pattern of all geographically different conflicts was fundamentally the same. For all disappearances carry within them the same despair. At that moment I needed *you*, Raphael. I could not go through all this shit on my own. It was simply too much for one person. Eventually the door opened and a nurse came in and she took me to my father.

Hektor stayed in intensive care for three days. A policeman guarded the door to his room. He had fallen into a coma just minutes before I arrived. Once or twice his eyes flickered open and I thought he recognised me. I tried talking to him, asking him about the ticket, the book. I tried telling him that Calypso would want him to give me an explanation, that his words might just save Aslam. I tried asking him where Lyle was. Counter Terrorism came in several times to sit with me. Once the man caught my eye and I felt rather than saw a glimmer of a smile hover behind his eyes. Or perhaps I just imagined it. We were on different sides of an invisible wall that forbade such things. And so I sat for three days, refusing food, utterly alone. On the third day the surgeon came. When he saw Counter Terrorism there he beckoned him outside. They were gone for about five minutes. When the surgeon returned he was accompanied by a nurse, a black woman with large eyes and a sympathetic face. The sight of her brought the ready tears to my eyes. I was faint with hunger. But I knew what was coming. The surgeon asked me if I would give permission to switch the machines off.

'We have very little electricity,' he said, apologetically. 'There are other people equally needy.'

He didn't say that Hektor would be a vegetable for the rest of his life but the implication was in his face. I agreed. There were children and pregnant women who badly needed the few doctors still working. So the machine was turned off. At least Hektor died peacefully.

I walked home through this new snowstorm, carrying Hektor's pathetic possessions. His worry beads, his car keys, his gold ring, his clothes and his shoes. For the third time I was in possession of objects belonging to the disappeared and the dead.

Everything was empty now. The street was empty of people

but with overflowing wheelie bins on the pavement. Organic matter lay rotting in the gutter. I heard Calypso's voice describing the moment she arrived home to find Aslam being handcuffed by the police.

My bag burst. And my cabbage rolled into the gutter like a head.

I was screaming the words in my head.

But they were from another life and once inside the house I stood uncertainly in the hall. The lights weren't working and there wasn't any heating. I walked into the kitchen. Everything belonging to those who had lived here was just as we had left them on that last day. The pans that had been washed by me stacked neatly one on top of the other. Washing-up liquid, a sponge, a dishcloth, a pair of rubber gloves. Seeing them, I started to shake uncontrollably. Here was a kitchen landscape without people, possessions without owners. Something was welling up inside me and what I did next had no name. Crying was not what that sound could be called. When I had finished, I sat for a long time on the floor, my head resting on a cupboard door, staring at my hands. Where could I go from here?

25.

Twenty-seven years have passed since that day, Raphael, and the blue ice now melts steadily. I am no longer the same person I was. What happened has left its indelible mark on me. The snow has stopped. It will never return. The harsh conditions and the permafrost that came down from the tundra of Russia through northern Scandinavia are retreating. The ice is buckling and cracking, large triangles are coming away from the high banks, dropping sharply and forming streams that lick and suck and expand. The ice disgorges water that in turn floods the land, pushing everything that stands in its way. I hear the insistent, sad sound of a desolate rain dripping from eaves and windowsills, hurrying restlessly along drains and underground waterways, following a path to the sea. New, astonishing wetlands form spontaneously all over the city. Lakes appear overnight, waterfalls cascade through long-forgotten rocks, white and foamy, and the winter silence is being broken by a thousand sounds of invisible fountains. The thaw is here, Raphael, and with it comes a tidal wave of memories that crash against me. And as the old things surface from the old life I feel my heart bend and crack like the ice. Try as I might I cannot stop the thoughts that now pour out. For underneath the drifts, the layers of melting ice, there is unfinished business I buried long ago. Preserved under ice, uncovered now, these thoughts begin to taunt me.

Remember, remember, the voices cry.

They will not go away but follow me around like a mournful dog. Peace evades me. There *is* no peace. No place to hide. You appear before me – you and all the others. Like revellers emerging after a party to dance before my eyes.

'Leave me be!' I cry.

But, no, you will not go away.

'What do you want from me?' I cry.

Do you remember, Raphael, how you once said, no winter lasts for ever? Well, the ice *is* melting but I feel no joy. Those of us left clinging to this raft of life have changed beyond recognition. Muslims, Jews and Christians have become simply names for outdated traditions. The irony of this is lost on most.

I live without expectations in the old house, sitting at the old kitchen table, sleeping in my old childhood bed. Like the bathroom cabinet that lies on the floor exactly where it was left, what has been broken cannot be fixed. Aslam's room has been closed for many years – there is no point going in there. Sometimes, when the mood takes me, I curl up in my parents' bed and sleep. But you could not call this living, Raphael.

I have closed the surface of my mind for years and these rising memories serve only to disturb me.

'Go away!' I cry. 'Leave me in peace.'

And a little later, watching the floodwater carrying ice floes, 'What unfinished business? There *is* no unfinished business …'

Or is there? It would seem this thaw has finally brought on the madness that I have shut out until now.

There is a man living in the house next door, a different one from the one who lived there when Calypso was alive. That man perished together with his family years ago. This new man is different and sometimes, when he sees me in the thawing garden feeding what few birds are returning, he comes over to talk to me. Yesterday he told me he'd heard that the last nightingale in the city had finally died.

'The nightingale is officially extinct,' he said.

I gave a small laugh. Really? What did I care?

'It survived these twenty-seven years only to die of shock over this thaw.'

I said nothing.

'But don't worry, Hera,' he continued, 'listen!'

And he stood on the other side of our still icy garden whistling the bird's song. So accurate was he that the other birds fell silent and an old mangy cat came out of the bushes, mouth twitching with hunger.

'I've made a recording of it,' my neighbour told me cheerfully. 'So that the song will live on, regardless.'

So proud was he of this achievement that he forgot for a moment that he was dying from the effects of frostbite. All that mattered was the nightingale's song living on; an extinct bird living through an extinct man and a machine. In some distant way I marvelled at such passion.

'How's your painting coming on?' he asked me.

I saw he wanted a conversation.

'Not bad,' I lied.

And then I went indoors.

I know this neighbour is lonely and frightened of dying alone. But for me intimacy remains painful.

And how can I tell him I spend most of the nights since the

ice began melting looking at the stars, searching the skies for some shred of comfort that never comes.

26.

Time, like the song of a wild bird, has flown and I am forty-seven now. Our twenty-seven-year winter is receding but still, try as I might, I cannot silence your voice. Would we recognise each other should we meet by chance?

'Speak to me, Raphael. Or if you cannot, then leave me alone!'

Sometimes in this new floating world of ice and clear rushing water I call your name over and over again as though I am praying.

'Was it you who said that water carries memory within it?'

The strength of this thaw astonishes me. I listen as it breaks up the frozen silence. But I am worn out with missing you. Like the refrigerated man I found the other day, embalmed in his car, I, too, have been kept on ice.

What is this receding white world doing to me?

A few days ago, as so often happens since the thaw began, it was the rain that woke me. Opening my eyes, I found myself asleep again on Calypso's side of the bed. I had no idea how I got there. Perhaps I sleepwalk back to the things I love? Disorientated, I panicked, struggling to remember the residue of a dream. I felt my chest tighten. My face was wet, my head throbbing. Water, I needed water. In my unfathomable dream

I knew there was a figure walking in the desert, searching for something, but beyond this I remembered nothing. The dream had taken possession of my voice. My body ached. I blinked but the act of looking was painful. This is more or less how I wake each morning since the blue ice started melting. My sleep is always filled with terror, my waking unrefreshed.

As sometimes happens, since the rain began falling, my anger flared up.

'How could you have been so cruel?' I cried once more.

And a little later, 'Only once did you say I was beautiful and even then it was with some reluctance. As if the words were wrenched from your mouth.'

I must stop talking to myself in this futile way, I told myself.

I opened the window and felt the rain fall gently on my face like a caress. It wasn't warm yet but the wind had dropped a little. I saw pools of water in the garden below. And dead grass. Since this thaw began I have had an ulcerated mouth and no appetite. Swallowing is painful and the cough that began a few months ago has got worse. I went downstairs into what was once my parents' living room. The room is damp, there are holes in the floorboards and the iced-up window is oozing rain now. I sat for a moment on the old sofa where Calypso had sat crying. The sofa sags in the middle; the stuffing escapes from it like despair. There is a broken television set in the corner of the room, a copy of the holy book, some worry beads. There is a newspaper with a faded image of my brother's face staring out. I closed my eyes. I have not been able to throw that newspaper away. I can't bear this room any more, I thought. It is a place of endless grief. How I have managed to live here for so long is a mystery to me. I shook my head and opened my eyes again and then I saw the last painting I worked on before I decided to stop painting altogether.

The painting is blue like the blue ice that is melting.

Blue like the future.

Blue like a thousand desert flowers after rain.

And blue like a night filled with a million stars.

But I cannot think of stars without weeping. I cannot think of blue without remembering your eyes.

27.

What is this thing that eats away at me with such terrible urgency? It is impossible to stay inside this house any longer. The noise of running water is too loud and the constant breaking and falling of ice hurts my head. It is as though there is construction work going on outside. It is impossible to get anything done feeling as I do. So I go outside to continue my conversation with you.

Why *did* you leave me, Raphael?

Did I not love you enough?

Was it that I was too young?

Was it because I was born a Muslim?

I need to know.

Since the thaw all I do is walk endlessly every day. I am restless and cannot be still. So I walk. From east to west, north to south, I cross and re-cross this overflowing, liquid city. Under arches I go, through doorways without doors. Walking between buildings emerging from the ice, past buried gardens where dead grass and leafless trees, still knee-deep in water, surface. Skirting the edges of newly formed wetland where I see rusting car bodies floating and bumping noisily against each other. The sky is pearly grey, reflected on the giant broken waterlilies of ice with a tender new light. And as I walk through this heritage of ruin the voices in my head grow louder. No one ever stops me on these walks. There is hardly anyone left and in any case those few people who do remain no longer stare. Partly this is because they are filled with their own stagnant apathy but also because I am of no interest. Those who remain have seen every combination of strangeness. There are no surprises. I am just a madwoman in black.

Yes, Raphael, the city is awakening at last. The river flows like a ribbon of mercury, its icy silence disappearing. Having been pared almost to the bone by man's stupidity, the city is being baptised afresh by water. And carried within these currents are the voices of the disappeared following me. Escape is impossible.

Yesterday, disturbed by another partly remembered dream, I had a sudden urge to visit the sea again. But it isn't possible to walk there and I remembered my dying neighbour had told me of a little-used driverless train that trundles up and down most days since the thaw.

'It travels to the coast,' the neighbour told me. 'Why don't you go there? They say the seagulls are returning. Go and see them for me.'

Recalling his words, I went to the old depot with its concrete buildings cracked by the weight of ice. And I waited. An hour passed. And another hour as I squatted on the ground. I felt faint. The voices in my head grew insistent and unbearable. Idly I noticed my left hand was bleeding. A beetle, wet from the downpour, slid drunkenly across the ground, hesitated and disappeared from view. The rain fell gently, intent on destroying the mounds of ice. It prised open fissures, poured into newly expanded gullies, probing and flowing into every crevice, its long fingers entering every hiding place and refusing to leave me alone. The whole landscape as far as the eye could see was a shimmer of glistening wetness. The light was liquid and beautiful. I stared dully ahead until suddenly I heard the slow rumbling that signalled the approaching train. The track glinted magically in the rain and I saw the train coming towards me in a mist of vapour. It was emptier than any ghost train at a fairground and just as pointless. When it stopped I wrenched open the door with my good hand and jumped in. Then, sitting on the hard green seat, I gazed out of the broken window. I was exhausted. The blood on my hand was clotting, my clothes were wet. The train waited a while as though its schedule demanded it and then it moved slightly, stopped and rattled onwards. We were off. Fields of ice heaped up in harvest sheaves appeared and disappeared on either side. We passed a house standing alone in one such field. It was an elegant house with fine, stuccoed fretwork and an Edwardian veranda. I saw a woman looking out of a window and our eyes met briefly in a shock of recognition. Then she, too, vanished and I was alone again. The train passed through a small town and the view changed once more. Here, the cranes stood motionless and disused. And now I saw a whitewashed mosque, its dazzling white minaret, like all minarets everywhere, utterly silent. I looked harder but saw only a world on the brink of extinction.

And then the sea appeared. When the train stopped I got off and stretched my legs. It was no longer raining, and here the air was warmer and the ice thinner. There were bare rowan trees bent with time and the wind. On the beach I breathed deeply and watched the waves tossing slabs of ice as

28.

A few nights after this day by the sea I decided to embark on an altogether different expedition. This time I planned to go to the old hospital. My neighbour has told me I can steal medicine here, to keep for the day when I will need it. My neighbour knows he will not last much longer and he wanted to advise me.

'Morphine is in short supply,' he said. 'You must steal as much as you can, enough to help you on your way when the time comes.'

So this is what I have been doing ever since the thaw began. As was usual, on this night I packed my small torch in my rucksack, along with a penknife and a hammer. Then out I went under the full moon to the swamp of melted ice where the hospital stands. There was no one around and the moon was brighter than my torch. I squelched through the slush that the rain had churned up, my face covered because of the fetid air. The thaw has been bringing up the corpses. At first they appeared in perfect condition but now, with the ice disappearing and the air warming up, they stink as they begin to rot. According to my neighbour disease is sure to follow.

As I walked, I noticed something glowing in the darkness. Was it an animal? Or the ghost of a poor dead soul emitting a phosphorescent light? The light blinked twice and I was reassured. It was only a silver fox, commonplace these days, though quite possibly rabid. I walked hurriedly on. In order to reach the old hospital I had first to pass through a multi-storey car park. The building is in a state of collapse without enough ice to prop it up. There were bodies floating in a tank of melted snow, shoes without feet, hubcaps and oil drums filled with crushed ice. The smell was terrible and I hurried on, my scarf held up to my nose. If one of the last remaining guards were to see me I knew I would be shot or at least knifed. I was, after all, intent on stealing.

On the other side of the car park was a group of dead pine trees, their leafless branches the colour of rust. The moon was busy silvering the world and I was reminded of the lights from all the obsolete computer screens in all the abandoned offices. A few frost-crippled leaves that had escaped the worst of the weather cast little shadows on the ground. I walked swiftly past a row of wooden posts jutting like rotten teeth from the soft mud. Once long ago there were allotments here. The former hospital loomed up and, with its broken windows, doors that swung noisily, wheelchairs that lay on their sides quietly rusting in cesspools of water, it was a place of shocking desolation. I went in through the main entrance and stopped. This was the most dangerous part of my journey because sometimes guards patrol the grounds. They are not guarding the hospital – they have no knowledge of the morphine or the other drugs that still remain here – they merely want to get out of the deadly air. I was intensely aware of every sound but tonight there was nothing except the slow, black drip of liquid from unseen rafters. I stepped on something soft and bloated and heard air leaking out of it. Suppressing a scream, I fled towards the building that was once a pharmacy. To get there I had to pass the empty neonatal clinic, the dialysis ward, the operating theatre, abandoned save for a table over which a circular light still hung. I had to pass the rows of cubicles with their 'Danger X-rays' signs and then out across a small open area, once a garden for the residents but now just a heap of melting ice. The pharmacy lay on the far side. My heart was beating fast; the stench was such that I almost vomited. As I approached the building, I thought I heard a noise. I stopped walking. But there was no one, only the sound of water dripping. As I crossed the ice garden with its broken wooden seats, I noticed that since my last visit the doors leading into the old pharmacy had disappeared. Someone else had discovered this place and had probably taken them to use as firewood. Worried, I wondered if they had also found the morphine. It was after all several weeks since my last visit.

But then I saw the boxes remained untouched, stacked amongst the piles of rubbish. My neighbour used to be the pharmacist here. It was he who left them like this years ago. Had he left the medicine in a cupboard others would have certainly helped themselves by now. As it is, no one knows about this little treasure trove. The boxes were too heavy and too large to carry back to my house and in any case I could not afford to attract any attention to myself. I might have easily been caught so I'd been siphoning off the drugs slowly, taking them back with me bit by bit.

I opened the largest box. Then I shone my torch on the syringes and the phials, the white packets of painkillers and antibiotics. Yes, it was all as before. I took my rucksack off my shoulders and started filling it. I worked fast. Like those of an addict my fingers trembled. The last time I was here I had

29.

'What are you doing here?' I gasped.

I don't know which of us was the more startled.

'*Raphael!*'

My voice was hoarse. In the moonlight your face was angelic; your hair, no longer dark, was instead silvery white against the doorway. Neither of us seemed able to move. I heard myself breathing very hard as I put my hand cautiously out. Something was glinting in the dark.

'What is it?' I whispered. 'Have you come back?'

There was no reply. My hand trembled. My whole body was shaking violently.

'*Raphael?*' My mouth was dry.

Then, without a sound, you turned swiftly and vanished from the room and, as you went, the small flying frog leapt through the air in a streak of fluorescent light, landing on your shoulder. The next moment the moon went behind a cloud and you were both swallowed up by the darkness. Unnerved, I bent to pick up my stolen goods and, shoving them back into the bag, I retreated.

I couldn't think straight. The walk back took longer than anticipated because I was so profoundly disturbed by what had just happened. Now I knew I was going mad.

'Was it you, Raphael?' I muttered. 'Or someone who looks like you?'

I couldn't stop shaking. In my headlong haste I came up against a new roadblock near the disused car park. Hardly able to function, I made a detour through a defrosting shopping mall and across to the bridge by the river. I was running now, slipping on the ice and water, falling over, panting. There wasn't a soul to be seen along the riverbank. The plates of ice have shrunk there now, the water grown vast; it smells terrible and is undoubtedly toxic. Without the moon and in the absence of electricity everything was of course cloaked in darkness. When the moon reappeared it was possible to see the Tower faintly outlined against the sky. The tattered flag was black against it but, although the ravens are long gone, the moat is filled with water. Usually I cannot pass by the Tower without stopping to think about Aslam but on this occasion I was too upset to do anything except hurry on. My knees were bleeding from the falls. Eventually I came towards the road and clambered up the embankment. I was thirsty. What I suspect is a thyroid problem makes me feel thirsty all the time.

I hurried on. There was no one on the road, just me, the night, and the vague sound of the river running below. I tried to concentrate. If it wasn't you, Raphael, then who did I see? I was both confused and stupidly hopeful. It couldn't possibly have been you – could it? I remembered the streak of yellow light as the frog leapt onto your shoulder and suddenly I realised I'd left my torch behind. I would have to go back for it. I wanted to go back *instantly* but I knew this would be unwise. I was filled with despair – but at least this proved I was still alive, I thought wildly.

It was well past midnight when I reached my house. For a minute I stood and stared at my neighbour's house, wanting desperately to talk to someone; *anyone*. And then without warning I was weeping all over again. For the cruel years that have passed and for all that I have lost.

'*Was* it you, Raphael? Have you come back? *Tell me*. Were you unable to keep away from me in the end?'

In the kitchen I lit the stove with twigs I had collected. Then I added wood and placed a kettle over the fire just as you used to, Raphael. I emptied my rucksack and in a frenzy of distress counted my syringes and phials of morphine.

'Tomorrow I shall go back for my torch,' I said out loud. 'Who cares about the guards? Tomorrow I will use a different route.'

The kettle was singing and, calmer now that I'd decided on a plan, I made myself a small pot of tea. Afterwards I went upstairs and fetched the first painting I made of you. It was from another time and place. Staring at it, there was no doubt in my mind, Raphael, that the man I had just seen was you.

30.

I was unable to return to the hospital for two whole days because I was ill, Raphael. For several days after seeing you I became delirious with a fever, possibly brought on by shock. Then the coughing started again. I dosed myself with the painkillers I had, knowing the way things were going for me. I started painting a little during this time but the longing to go back to the hospital did not go away. I wasn't hungry and so didn't eat but this in turn left me feeling weak. I took to sitting in the kitchen with the back door wide open. I had not done such a thing for many years. Sitting there, watching the garden reappearing through water, I wrote a list of all the things I would never have.

I will never have children

I will never know what it is to walk fearlessly down a street

Or have a friend

Or trust another person

Or write a letter

Or eat fresh vegetables

Or freshly slaughtered spring lamb.

Snowdrops are a thing of the past.

As is birdsong

And roses, although they say that might change in a few weeks.

But I never believe anything *they* say.

Perhaps the worst thing of all is that I will never know the whole story.

I have missed you terribly, Raphael. I missed Calypso, too. You are never too old to miss your mother but it is you that I could not forgive.

It was a beautiful November day with the pastel radiance of a new spring. Staring out into the garden, I noticed an old rose bush planted long ago by Hektor. I went across to it, my feet sinking into the oozing mud, and saw, with an unbearable sense of loss, that it had survived the long winter. How was this possible?

'I want the roses to bloom again,' I cried.

The words were wrenched out of me.

'I don't want the world to die.'

On the afternoon of the following day I felt a little better. And that settled it.

'This evening I *will* go to the hospital,' I told myself. 'If a guard finds me, the worst that would happen is they'd kill me. Better a swift death than this limbo.'

I was reluctant to admit to myself that it was you I was hoping to see because, by now, I had convinced myself I had imagined everything and that the beginning of the fever had been responsible for my hallucination. There had to be a logical explanation for my craziness, I felt sure. Having come to a decision, feeling a little less agitated, I decided to visit the baker who owns the bread shop. I hadn't seen him for some time. When he saw me he smiled.

'Where've you been?' he asked. 'Look at you! You look like a skeleton.'

This man bakes his bread in one of the last remaining wood ovens. I told him I hadn't been hungry and I told him about my fever. I didn't mention seeing you of course, Raphael. He would have thought I'd really gone mad.

'That's no good,' he says. 'You'll fade away.'

'Well, today there's been a little sunshine,' I said.

'Better get used to more of that!' he said a touch grimly. 'Don't think this thaw will go on for ever.'

Then he looked sad and gave me my loaf of bread. It was peasant bread, coarsely milled, brown, delicious and still hot from the oven. In the middle of our twenty-first century, Raphael, how is it that we live in such pre-medieval hardship?

'Pity we have no butter,' he said.

No cows, no butter, we both shrugged. At least this baker still has one last sack of closely guarded flour.

But when it goes?

'You're too thin,' he scolded. 'It isn't good. At least eat my bread.'

'Well, eating alone isn't all that interesting,' I said and he nodded, understandingly.

His wife had died years ago when the blizzard was at its worst.

'There is no God,' he said, raising his hands skywards. 'He has gone elsewhere to a more deserving planet.'

He laughed. Once he had been a devout Jew. Now he says he is without a soul.

'Who needs a soul in a place like this?' he joked.

A woman walked past. She wore the hijab but she wasn't necessarily a Muslim woman. Both men and women veil themselves if the mood takes them. No one really cares about such things any more. The churches are empty too, as are those other places of worship – the banks. Those who once believed in their gods look uneasily up at the sky, wondering when it will all be over.

'Come back soon,' the baker said after the woman was out of view.

He is a lovely man. For centuries his relatives have been persecuted so we share the empathy of the survivor. The dead are silent for the moment and the living have lost their voices. Pain, as you well know, Raphael, does that to people.

'We live amongst the broken threads of other people's lives,' the baker called out after me as if reading my thoughts.

I nodded. And then I went.

Evening came at last. The vigilantes always have their meal at the same time each evening. They light fires at dusk and begin to roast the meat they've stolen during the day. As usual no thought is given to what they will do once even these poor animals become extinct. The inability to plan for what little future is left is amazing. They are broken individuals turned aggressive in their need to survive.

By the time I reached the hospital, because of the necessary but tedious detours, it was almost ten o'clock. I walked cautiously through the main entrance, avoiding the rotting corpses and slipping in a pool of some sticky substance. I shuddered. All around me were piles of computer printouts of hearts that had stopped beating, strewn everywhere. A light breeze started up, lifting the corner of my headscarf, and somewhere in the distance a door banged. I jumped but nothing else happened so I hurried out through the back entrance, stumbling over a wheelchair and almost missing a step. The enormous moon had again disappeared behind a cloud and without it or my torch everything was suddenly pitch black. Then an eerie sound echoed across the overgrown quadrangle and I froze. Had I not known it was impossible, I would have said that the sound was an owl calling. But there are no owls any longer. I crossed to the pharmacy, up more steps and in through the open doorway. On the wall was a torn poster that I hadn't noticed before. *Spring Is Almost Here* it stated and underneath was a child's drawing of a tree in blossom. I frowned, momentarily distracted. My heart was racing. There was no sign of you, Raphael. There was no sign of my torch either.

I looked around nervously. Maybe I'd dropped my torch along the riverbank or maybe I'd lost it on the road. I peered into the darkness, not knowing what to do next. Having hoped against all hope that I would see you, Raphael, I had to admit that now I was bitterly disappointed.

'Fool!' I said out loud and the word came back as an echo. *Fool, fool, fool!*

A piece of rotting timber fell from the rafters, followed by a rush of melted ice. I was soaked again. But I didn't care.

Memories flooded the surface of my mind. I was almost crying. Did you know, Raphael, that Hektor died in this hospital? And it was to the mortuary that Calypso was brought? Did I ever tell you? I shook my head.

'What's the point?' I said out loud. 'There is nothing here.'

Dejected, I turned around and began walking back towards the main entrance. And that was when I saw a pinprick of light ahead. Catching my breath, I drew back to stand completely still but the light was receding. And as I stared at it I saw that it was a torch being held in someone's hand. I took in the stooped shoulders, the dim outline and, without thinking, I screamed.

'*Raphael!*'

At that the figure stopped, half turning towards me. A second later the light was extinguished and all was darkness once more.

31.

In a blinding flash, shocked, I understood what I had not seen before, what I had, in my distress, failed to do and what I could no longer ignore. How had I forgotten? And as if on cue the moon appeared, shining in through the broken hospital. It was no ordinary moon but the last moon of this last season. We used to say, when the blue moon appeared it would bring to light the washed-up broken things from the absent lives that would never return again.

That time had come and in that moment I knew what I must do; what I have not dared in all these years. I needed to visit your old house, Raphael, twenty-seven years after I last set foot in it. Had you come to lead me there?

32.

The night was velvet and still. No dripping water, no chill wind. Even the old ice made no creaking noise as the last blue moon of the decade glided back into view. Silently it crossed the sky, treading its ancient path, shedding its traveller's light on our pitiful city. It was larger than life and twice as bright. Why had I thought there was a need for torchlight on such a night as this?

My heart rose. I was with you again at last. Oh, Raphael!

'I am here,' I said out loud, but you were already ahead of me, hurrying on, your back turned away.

'I am ready, Raphael,' I said. 'I shall follow you without fear.'

You once told me that all mankind was born for a purpose. Once that purpose is over we die. Fleetingly I wondered if your purpose here tonight was simply to help me find the answers I craved. To help me to find peace. You were walking fast and the moonlight followed you, resting on your hair like a benediction.

It was quite a trek. We passed by a dark glacial lake, covered in some sort of algae. Had you not been with me I would have fallen into it but instead we skirted around the edges. I had no idea you could walk so fast and I struggled to keep up. At some point you stopped and held your hand up, listening, but then walked on again. You did not turn back, or acknowledge me in any other way but I was content to let you lead. After what seemed like an hour, we left the lake and emerged out through a spinney of dead, matchstick-thin trees onto an abandoned dual carriageway. I tried to figure out where on earth we were but the land was so destroyed it was impossible to identify anything. I shook my head, confused. The moon disappeared and we now passed the entrance to an underground tunnel. All names were erased. You walked hurriedly on, sure-footed and certain. I was sweating under my headscarf. And then, without warning, we came to a high, broken wall. The moon reappeared but I couldn't see you. There was the sound of a gate being opened and I saw a gaping hole in the wall.

Now we were in a wooded area. I was astonished. I knew that strange things happened during our winter of twenty-seven years, that not every living thing died. Perhaps this wood grew during that time. And there before me was the house, your house, the place where all my dreams lived. The same dark-red door, the same lace curtains. A wheelie bin, discoloured and broken, stood beside the back gate; the number painted on it had long since faded but the bin itself remained.

It isn't love that will survive but plastic, you said once, teasing me. But you were wrong, Raphael.

I crossed the threshold like a sleepwalker and stared around me. Here were the cold ashes from a long-forgotten fire. Here were the cups I drank from, the plates on which we ate. The table exactly as before. There were wine-encrusted sediments resting like jewels in the bottom of each cup. Which one touched your lips? And which mine? Time and the devil had wrought little change on the scene. I stretched out my hand and the lace curtain crumbled into the dust of fairy tales. A shrivelled pomegranate, looking as if it had been in a pharaoh's tomb, rested on the table. Unable to cope, I sat on a dusty chair in the middle of the room. It was a second before I realised *why* the chair was there. In *that* position, on *that* spot, underneath the light. My heart was thumping hard and I began to shake once more. But I didn't cry yet. I saw the cat's bowl, the flowerless vase, the poster of a universe I no longer recognised. There was a map of your home, the salt desert light still clearly visible.

And I recalled, in slow motion, what, returning after that single night we spent together, I found.

You, Raphael. Here. In this spot. Hanging from the ceiling. Held by a knot. Tied securely to death.

Did you *hear* my scream?

Do you know how you looked to my horrified eyes, that for me you were like some macabre drawing? Lifeless, speechless, still turning slowly, a solitary leaf on a winter branch. Both yourself, and not yourself.

'Why, Raphael? *Why did you do it?*'

It was your shoes I saw first: brown, scuffed, old, worn, size eights.

'Oh, let me have those shoes so I can wear them to the end of the journey that is my life.'

I ask you now: did you walk across the desert in those shoes looking for Ishtar? Searching in the dust and amongst the rocks and pin-sharp stars for any small trace of calcium you might find? Never finding it, yet never ending your search?

That morning, your shoes swung to the beat of some secret music. Would you have danced the tango in this way, in the past, Raphael? Would you have twirled and swung Ishtar in this way, laughing? Answer me!

I don't remember what I saw next. The chair, perhaps, overturned?

And now comes the hardest part of all.

I must write it down and speak it out loud.

I must cry it from the rooftops

And scream it out to the sea.

When they came to take you down from the ceiling, they found it difficult. You had tied the knot so firmly.

'This one wanted to go,' I heard one of them say, grimly.

And afterwards, not recognising me, apologetically: 'You okay, miss? Sit down, you've had a shock.'

No, I thought, you know nothing about my shocks.

What shocked me was what *you* had taken from me. That I, who had lost everything, should lose you, too, was too much to bear. How cruel you have been to me, Raphael. You took the last word from my mouth and left me speechless. Now all I have is the cup, the belt and the shoelace. Is this fair? How could you have forgotten that final hour we spent together?

There was a small piece in the newspaper about you the next day.

Vagrant hangs himself.

It hurts me still that you were called a vagrant. Lyle, the only person I could talk to, was gone, in search of Aslam. To save what could not be saved. Another useless task in a lifetime of useless tasks.

'Don't you have somewhere to go, miss?' the policeman asked.

He still did not recognise me. Possibly it was the veil that confused him. But no, I shook my head, I had nowhere to go.

'Why, Raphael? Why?'

My thoughts were echoing around the empty room and then I noticed the bedroom door was ajar. Had there been someone else here? Cautiously I went in and what I saw was a bed with clothes that crumbled at my touch. A frosted-over mirror in which I caught a glimpse of my younger face.

'Why, Raphael, why? Why didn't you wait?'

This was the question I kept asking out loud. Did you know there was an avalanche that day, Raphael, that destroyed my heart?

'Answer me, damn you! Was it Ishtar who called you back? Did I mean so little to you?'

The room was silent as a tomb, no ticking clock, no breath to move the air. You gave me no answer so I asked again.

Why didn't you give me a chance? Oh, *Raphael!* It was you who finished me off. Oscillating between anger and despair, I asked, why didn't you wait?

Moonlight crept slyly in through the window. It fell across the carpetless floor, the rotting boards, the broken hinges everywhere. And in a moment of illumination I saw what I didn't see before. There it was, tucked amongst the faded things on the mantelpiece.

Addressed to me in your hand.

Hera.

33.

I cannot love again, you had written.

To love is to be a hostage to fortune, to love is to take what chance comes your way and I am no longer a gambling man. Last night when you loved me with such eager desire, trust in your eyes, certainty too, I saw the evening star in your face.

Ishtar; my evening star. I had found you again. The poet Rilke said it is our ultimate task to love another person and foolishly I let you enter my heart. You have peeled away the hardness of the years, you have softened these last days and I have waited for your visits with longing. Foolishly, even though to love again was not my wish, I did these things. For, possessing all the stubbornness of the young, you were stronger than I was, Hera.

When I tried to beat you away you refused to go.

When I turned my face away from you your eyes would often fill with tears.

At other times I made you angry and this was easier for me to bear.

Worst of all were the times of silent acceptance on your part.

I cursed you, called you temptress, felt possessed by you and still you came back, never wavering in your generosity and your love.

Hera, you deserve a better man than I am. Someone young, like you. Someone who can take up the great challenges that will face our White City.

Forgive me. I am too broken to walk along that road with you.

Yesterday, before you arrived, I answered the door to the postman. What he held in his hand had taken many years to reach me. Years when sand and rock and dust were sifted. Years of painstaking searches with only hands and an occasional trowel as tools. Backbreaking work that left no stone unturned on the desert plateau of my youth. Years spent dodging the militia who guarded that vast burial pit. Guided only by the mythical alicanto bird whose strange eyes emitted a luminous light.

All this was done for me as promised. There were times when I thought the promise had been forgotten, years when my dream of finding this treasure remained just that – a dream. Times when I would close my eyes in despair, longing for the unattainable. It was in this state of partly living that you stumbled across me and with your paints tried to make sense of who I am. And last night I let you in. I let you glimpse my story.

Last night, when you came to me with the rush of grief gushing from you like an open wound, pain like forked lightning on your face, I no longer could withstand you. I was caught off guard and then I saw with terrible certainty how it would be. I cannot follow you into the

247

dark, dark wood that has become your life. The road
that leads to enlightenment can only be travelled alone,
querida. And I who have walked that path cannot walk
it again. Only in the fairy tales meant for children is it
possible to love again. And so, I leave you. But one last
gift before I go. I leave you this. It is an index to the
violence of human history. Keep it close for, with it in
your hand, you hold the stars. You hold the disappeared.
In your hand that which has gone returns. May it be
your talisman during the years ahead and may you be
the sole witness to the muffled discourse of my past.

War teaches the human animal nothing better,
querida, than how to kill, maim and torture one
another with greater imagination, greater ease and
greater indifference. This is the legacy of Hitler.

Raphael

I stare at the letter. What gift? A sound makes me look up and
here it is on your kitchen table. The police had not told me. I
had not seen it before. It has taken years but at last it is mine.

Stunned, I turn to you. I have so many questions. But you
are nowhere in sight. A dam bursts somewhere deep inside
me. Here it is then, so small, so inconspicuous, surviving
not just the elements but also the years. This spent token of
some individual existence, delicate as a Brancusi sculpture,
lying in the palm of my hand. A sliver, a fragment, of
what? A thighbone, bleached silver by the desert sun. A last
distinguishing trace of a vanished life, giving up its story.

A sole surviving vestige.

A cherished part of that someone.

A voice without sound, a language without words.

Coming home, begging to be heard. At last.

Ishtar, you had written. Ishtar. The evening star. So you found her in the end, Raphael. The gravitational force of memory has returned.

You and I and Ishtar, together at last.

'But, Raphael,' I cry, 'did I have no say in all of this?'

Outside, a spring breeze has started up. It blows the dust across the room. Something rustles quietly. Perhaps it is the figure of you disappearing for the final time. The moon has moved away and there are shooting stars in sight. All around me the Milky Way rides high above the city. It spins its light across this cursed land of ours. And I ask myself, have I always been in love with a ghost or am I the ghost?

34.

It is over now and I alone am left.

Calypso went long ago, as did Hektor.

And so did you.

Lyle has left this world, too.

I keep your gift to me, the small bone, on a table by my bed. It is white, like heat. White like the city. One day soon, when I am over the shock of reading your letter, I shall put it to rest in the earth.

There is one other thing that I would like to do. I would like to visit the sea for the last time. If water carries memories I shall sit beside it and think of you and Ishtar, and little Helen too. Breasting the waves, all together, laughing, unaware of the years ahead.

Until the end I shall continue to live in the boarded-up house on whose front step Calypso collapsed. I shall sweep the dust from behind its doors.

And think of my brother Aslam.

Occasionally I will hear his gentle voice like a long-lost echo.

You know, Hera, he will say, *a century ago every single Muslim country was ruled by non-Muslims. Of course this has had an effect on the world. How could it not?*

'Aslam,' I whisper now as I walk the streets of the city. 'Where are you?'

The sun does not forget a village just because it is small, he replies.

One night I dreamed that he handed me an apple. It was exactly the size and weight of a human heart.

Go on, eat it, was his answer. *So that our collective sins can be remembered.*

'What am I doing in this world?' I asked my dream-brother.

Haven't you noticed how in the winter the faces of the people on the street make you think they've just failed an exam? was his laughing answer.

My dream-brother's face is etched in madness.

But these moments of sleep conversation are rare, Raphael. Mostly the place is silent.

I must tell you that, two years ago, word came from Lyle, his voice distant and strained.

'No, I didn't actually see him,' he admitted.

The security apparently was unbelievable, Raphael. And the weather made it impossible to reach the Arena easily. Lyle visited as often as he could. He had lived for a while in a small boarding house overlooking the sea.

'I'm not leaving,' he told me. 'There aren't any flights operating. I could try to get a passage on a cargo ship but I think I'd rather stay here for the time being. Until his trial.'

Aslam's trial was without jury, Raphael, and with no lawyer to represent him. It was a closed court, the verdict unknown until it was all over. It was the way the Arena operated.

'They call it democracy,' Lyle told me, his voice faint. 'Have you heard of this word?'

The phone went blank then. Someone had cut him off. Mobile phones barely worked any more.

When he next rang, several weeks had passed. The line was bad; I couldn't work out what he was saying.

'What happened at the hearing?' I shouted.

Silence.

'I wrote a love letter to Calypso,' he said at last. 'In it I affirmed my love for her again. I kept it with me for a long time and then, finally, yesterday I posted it. Probably it will never arrive.'

I imagined I could hear the sea in the background, but it was probably just the bad line. Before he rang off he said the hearing had been postponed.

Aslam never came back, Raphael.

No.

His skeleton was packed into a sealed container and given to Lyle. It weighed nothing.

'Sorry about this,' the deliveryman had said. 'I believe he starved to death.'

He'd looked apologetic. When they had come to clean the building after the prison was closed down they found Aslam bent double and in a corner of his cell.

Aslam's orange jumpsuit had turned to dust, along with his flesh.

Only the calcium from his bones had kept his skeleton in one piece.

The deliveryman asked Lyle to sign for the box. He would not leave without a signature. It was more than his job was worth, he told him.

Lyle did not return to the White City, Raphael. There were no planes that could fly such distances.

'I, too, shall die here,' he told me on one of his disjointed phone calls. 'Like my son I shall starve to death.'

You know, I think the intense heat and what they did to Aslam finally drove Lyle insane.

Was my brother guilty of any crime?

Not of the things they accused him of.

Aslam could not have hurt a fly. There was no proof, but in any case those who controlled his fate needed no proof.

'In the end,' Lyle told me, in his very last phone call, 'we shall all return to dust.'

I did not tell him what had happened to me, Raphael. I did not tell him what you did or how it broke me. These days I just stroke the small shard of bone you left and think of you all.

Now the snow and ice have almost gone, Raphael. There is new growth struggling to survive.

I am no longer young, for that time has passed.

Our pendant world hangs precariously on its golden chain waiting for its new beginning.

Tonight when the sun sinks once more into the sea the moon will shine its silvery light across the land. And in this small pause a sense of hope will hover once more over the world. But only for those yet to be born. It is they who will pick up the threads of the new era.

As for me, Raphael, it is far too late. Tomorrow, and during the few tomorrows left to me, I shall continue to walk the city, iridescent and lovely in its new spring dawn. And I can tell you now, with all the certainty of the winters past, that despite everything that has happened, though you could not wait for me, rest assured, my love for you has not been destroyed. It remains intact, glowing more brightly with the passing years; surviving.

Acknowledgements

I would like to thank my agent Robert Dinsdale for his vision and his understanding.

I would like to thank my publisher, Jane Aitken at Gallic, for believing in *The White City* from the very beginning. Pilar Webb for her close scrutiny of the text, Emily Boyce who knew my writing from a previous novel and Jimena Gorraez-Connolly for her encouragement, not least for all things Mexican.

I would also like to thank the rest of the Gallic team working invisibly on my behalf.

I would like to thank the Chilean refugees who talked to me so openly about their shocking experiences at the hands of Pinochet. I am not allowed to use their names but *they* were the inspiration for this book.

Finally I would like to thank my family who watched from the sidelines as *The White City* took shape.

Thank You